"I'd watch wh
under a full moon, if I were you."

As if to underscore his meaning, Delaney's eyes traveled the length of Hannah's pale silk wrapper—a slow and keen appraisal.

Hannah's shoulders stiffened and her chin came up. "I'll wear what I choose, Sheriff, and when I choose. How others react to that isn't my concern."

He shifted the shotgun slightly. The grim set of his mouth eased into a small smile. "That's a fine notion, ma'am, and if you lived in a fairy-tale castle, I guess it would suffice. But you wander around like that here—" he angled his head, indicating her wrapper "—and you best be prepared to deal with the consequences."

"Consequences!" Hannah was furious, rising from her perch on the railing as if it had caught fire. Why, the man was clearly accusing her of out-and-out seduction…!

Dear Reader,

Heroes come in many forms, as this month's books prove—from the roguish knight and the wealthy marquess to the potent gunslinger and the handsome cowboy.

Longtime Harlequin Historical author Mary McBride has created a potent gunslinger-turned-sheriff in *The Marriage Knot,* and has given her hero a flaw: a wounded hand. With his smooth, almost shy demeanor and raw masculinity, Delaney is irresistible. He's also reliable and in love (only he doesn't know it yet), which is why old Ezra Dancer wills his house—and his young widow—to Delaney for safekeeping.

You *must* meet Will Brockett, the magnetically charming wrangler who uncharacteristically finds his soul mate in the tomboy who's loved him from afar, in *A Cowboy's Heart* by Liz Ireland. Fans of roguish knights will adore Ross Lion Sutherland and the lovely female clan leader he sets his sights on in *Taming the Lion,* the riveting new SUTHERLAND SERIES medieval novel by award-winning author Suzanne Barclay.

Rounding out the month is Nicholas Stanhope, the magnificent Marquess of Englemere in *The Wedding Gamble,* a heart-wrenching Regency tale of duty, desire—and danger—by newcomer and Golden Heart winner Julia Justiss.

Whatever your tastes in reading, you'll be sure to find a romantic journey back to the past between the covers of a Harlequin Historicals® novel.

Sincerely,

Tracy Farrell
Senior Editor

Please address questions and book requests to:
Harlequin Reader Service
U.S.: 3010 Walden Ave., P.O. Box 1325, Buffalo, NY 14269
Canadian: P.O. Box 609, Fort Erie, Ont. L2A 5X3

MARY McBRIDE

THE MARRIAGE KNOT

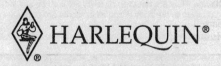

HARLEQUIN®

TORONTO • NEW YORK • LONDON
AMSTERDAM • PARIS • SYDNEY • HAMBURG
STOCKHOLM • ATHENS • TOKYO • MILAN • MADRID
PRAGUE • WARSAW • BUDAPEST • AUCKLAND

ISBN 0-373-29065-9

THE MARRIAGE KNOT

This edition published by arrangement with Harlequin Books S.A.

® and TM are trademarks of the publisher. Trademarks indicated with
® are registered in the United States Patent and Trademark Office, the
Canadian Trade Marks Office and in other countries.

Look us up on-line at: http://www.romance.net

Printed in U.S.A.

Books by Mary McBride

Harlequin Historicals

Riverbend #164
Fly Away Home #189
The Fourth of Forever #221
The Sugarman #237
The Gunslinger #256
Forever and a Day #294
Darling Jack #323
Quicksilver's Catch #375
Storming Paradise #424
The Marriage Knot #465

Harlequin Books

Outlaw Brides
"The Ballad of Josie Dove"

MARY McBRIDE

is a former special education teacher who lives in St. Louis, Missouri, with her husband and two young sons. She loves to correspond with readers, and invites them to write to her at: P.O. Box 411202, St. Louis, MO 63141.

For Joan C. Gunter
with affection and deep appreciation.

Prologue

Kansas, 1880

Until the morning Ezra Dancer shot himself, not much had happened in Newton. The railroad had come through in 1871, and for one wild summer the town was full of cowboys and longhorns, gamblers and quacks and whores. Newton was as sinful then as any Sodom or Gomorrah, but that honor—along with the cowboys and longhorns, the gamblers, quacks and whores—had long since passed west with the railroad to Dodge City.

Newton's makeshift tents and rickety shacks had been replaced with painted clapboard and solid brick. Most of the saloons had given way to drier businesses—Kelleher's Feed and Grain, the Merchant's Bank, the First Methodist Church—and where Madam Lola's canvas and cardboard brothel once had been, the citizens had built themselves a school.

As in most law-abiding towns, there was a jail for anyone who crossed the line, and there was a sheriff with a tough reputation to insure that nobody did.

Delaney.

His name was rarely spoken solo. Likely as not, it was mentioned in the same sentence as the Earps—Wyatt and Virgil and Morgan—and that reprobate dentist, Doc Holliday. But when the Earps and Holliday departed Kansas for the warmer clime and hotter prospects of Arizona in the autumn of '79, Delaney stood alone.

Or, to be more exact, he lay alone on a cot in a back room of the U.S. Marshall's office in Dodge City.

"Too bad you can't come with us," Morgan Earp had said in all sincerity, his eyes deliberately averted from Delaney's wounded arm.

"He will, I expect, as soon as he mends," Doc had said. "Isn't that so, Delaney?"

Although he had nodded a grim yes to Doc, Delaney hadn't followed them to Arizona after all, but had come—bad arm and a worse disposition—to Newton instead. And not a lot had happened in the six months since he'd taken the job of sheriff. There had been a brawl or two, and one domestic dispute that involved a horsewhip and a kitchen knife. But there hadn't been a shooting until the morning Ezra Dancer put a gun to his head and pulled the trigger.

When his deputy awoke him with the news, Delaney's first thought—like a searing bolt of lightning through his brain—was not about the deceased, but rather about the man's wife.

No. Not a wife anymore.

Hannah Dancer was a widow now.

That notion shook Delaney to his core.

Chapter One

It was seven-thirty in the morning, already warm and promising pure Kansas heat, when Delaney walked the half mile out to Moccasin Creek where Ezra Dancer's body had been discovered. A small group of men had already gathered under a big cottonwood, casting sidelong glances at the corpse, shrugging, pointing here and there before jamming their hands helplessly in their pockets and toeing the ground with their boots.

"Mornin', Sheriff," several of them murmured when Delaney joined their midst. He merely nodded in reply, his gaze immediately taking in the well-trodden terrain around the deceased. These old boys had probably been out here, shrugging and scratching their heads and feeling glad to be alive, since dawn, and while they were speculating on life in general and Dancer's death in particular, their big boots had been crushing the grass and stomping out whatever possible footprints or evidence of foul play there might have been.

"Damned shame if you ask me," Hub Watson said, swatting his hat against his leg. "Damned shame. What do you think, Sheriff?"

Delaney squatted down beside Ezra Dancer's body, his sawed-off shotgun balanced across his knees. What did he think? He thought he'd seen enough death to last him several lifetimes and enough bloodshed to color his disposition, and even his soul, a deep crimson. He thought he was getting very tired of death, particularly the notion of his own, especially now that his arm had failed him. Bone tired. And he thought Ezra Dancer must've been ten kinds of fool and a coward to boot to stick a pistol in his mouth and fire it.

There was no question that it was Dancer—half his face was still intact—and not a doubt that the man had killed himself deliberately while he reclined against the rough trunk of the cottonwood. His pose seemed quite relaxed even now while his finger was stiff around the trigger. And damned if Delaney didn't perceive half a hint of a smile on the man's still lips.

"Ezra's been very sick," somebody said. "He took a turn for the worse just yesterday."

Delaney glanced up to see Abel Fairfax, one of the boarders at the Dancers' house, a man in his early fifties, about the same age as the deceased.

"Sick? I didn't know that," Delaney said, but even

as he spoke the words he envisioned the difference six months had made in Dancer.

When Delaney had first come to town last December, Dancer—bushy-haired and barrel-chested—had come up to him at the Methodist lemonade social and pumped his wounded arm with such gusto that Delaney had had to grit his teeth to keep from screaming. And then there'd been that day in January when Dancer had taken a tumble on the icy street and Delaney just happened by in time to haul his bulky body out of the way of a wagon.

He studied the corpse now and realized that Dancer had probably dropped forty or fifty pounds in the past six months. There wasn't so much blood on him that he couldn't discern that Ezra's belt was buckled two notches tighter than usual. The man's hair appeared much grayer than Delaney recalled. It was pretty obvious that Dancer had been ill. But, of course, Delaney knew he hadn't noticed that because, all truth to tell, he'd spent the last few months going out of his way to avoid Ezra Dancer.

No. Not Ezra.

Ezra's wife.

"Somebody'll have to tell Hannah."

Whoever made that somber declaration, though, obviously wasn't volunteering.

Delaney pried the pistol from Dancer's cold grasp, checked to make sure the chambers were empty, then stood up.

"I guess that's my job," he said. "One of you men

want to tell the undertaker to come out here and re-
trieve the body?''

"Sure, Sheriff.'' Hub Watson spun on his heel,
slapped his hat on and trotted back to town.

Delaney stood there a moment longer, wishing he
were somewhere, someone else. He didn't much rel-
ish telling women their men were dead. He'd always
thought that the day would come when he'd be the
bearer of that lethal news to Mattie about Wyatt, or
to Lou when Morgan's number was up. He suspected
sometime in the future he still might have to do just
that.

It was one of the reasons he'd never remarried or
even gotten all that close to any woman. Not since
he'd come back from the war to discover that the
sweet girl he'd wed on the eve of his departure had
hanged herself on hearing the news—wrong, as it
turned out—that every soldier in Company H had
been killed at Chickamauga. It wasn't fair, not in the
soldiering business or in the job of carrying out the
law, to put a woman in that kind of jeopardy.

Hell, maybe he'd just never loved anybody the way
that Wyatt and Morgan did, he thought. Maybe to
them it was worth the risk. But once he joined up
with the Earps again, Delaney knew he'd still probably be bringing bad news to Mattie or Lou one of
these years.

But he never dreamed he'd be bringing such bad
news to Hannah Dancer. And if he *had* dreamed it,

he thought now, then he'd surely go to hell for merely entertaining the notion.

"Well, what do you say, Sheriff?"

Delaney had been so lost in his thoughts he hadn't even realized that Abel Fairfax had spoken to him. "Pardon?"

"I said I'll come along to the Dancer place with you. This is gonna be awful hard on Hannah." Fairfax shook his gray head, repeating, "awful hard on her, purely awful."

Delaney sighed as he stuck Ezra Dancer's pistol into his belt, then settled his own weapon against his thigh. "I'd be much obliged for your help, Abel. Guess there's no use in putting it off, is there?"

The older man shrugged, turning his gaze toward town. "Nope. No use."

Delaney sighed again, then said, "Let's go."

The Dancers' property took up a whole square block, nearly an acre of elm trees and shady grass and sunlit gardens. Ezra, or so the story went, had made his fortune outfitting—and perhaps even outwitting— hordes of gold-seekers in California back in the fifties. The house in Newton was said to be an exact replica of his previous abode in San Francisco, complete with arched doors and windows, fancy Greek columns, and fat, hand-carved balusters on the wide wraparound porch.

There was enough gingerbread on the building to decorate an entire village. Every outside nook and cranny was filled with some carved doodad or other. Even the trim had trimming of its own.

It was the damnedest house Delaney had ever seen. Not that he'd spent a lot of time looking at it, though. Whenever he passed by, on foot or on horseback, he trained his gaze elsewhere. Away. He was a practical man, if nothing else. Far from a dreamer, he saw no use in looking at what—or who—he couldn't have.

"Well, Ezra won't be climbing these anymore," Abel Fairfax said as the two men made their way up the broad front steps. When one of the boards groaned beneath their feet, he added, "Hannah's going to have to find herself a decent handyman now, I guess."

Delaney didn't respond. He'd never been inside this imposing residence before, and quite suddenly he felt as if he should have soaped up some after awakening that morning or at least put on a fresh shirt instead of the one he'd been wearing all week. He passed his fingertips along his jaw, vaguely wishing he had shaved.

Fairfax pulled open the screen door and motioned with one hand. "After you, Sheriff."

Delaney stepped over the threshold and damned if the temperature didn't feel as if it had dropped a dozen degrees in the distance of those few feet. The vestibule in which he found himself was papered in green brocade and dappled by sunshine pouring through the fanlight and through a stained glass window on the landing just ahead.

He took in a long breath, sweetened by eucalyptus

and cloves and maybe a tad of cinnamon. Until now, the finest place he'd ever seen had been Corina White's fancy house in Fort Smith. Compared to that, the Dancer house looked like Buckingham Palace. He glanced down at his boots, knowing they weren't shiny, but hoping at least they weren't clotted with dirt and that his spurs weren't tearing up the Persian carpet.

He heard soft conversation to his right, then looked into the dining room where the plump little schoolteacher and the thin fellow who worked at the bank— both of them boarders here at the Dancers'—sat across from each other at a large table, sipping coffee and taking bites of toast. It was still breakfast time. The thought surprised Delaney. He felt as if he'd been up half the day already.

"Hannah usually doesn't come down till nine or so." Abel Fairfax stood at the foot of the staircase, craning his neck upwards as if he could look around the landing and down the hallway on the second floor. "Hannah," he called softly. "Hannah, are you up?"

Delaney checked the big inlaid clock on the vestibule's far wall. It tinkled out a quarter chime just then. Eight-fifteen. Maybe Hannah Dancer was still asleep. Maybe he'd go on back to the jailhouse, have a cup of coffee and collect himself, then return in half an hour or so. Or maybe…

"Yes, Abel. I'm up."

Her voice preceded her down the staircase like a warm, luxurious breeze.

"What in the world is going on at this hour of the morning?" A tiny trill of laughter—like the music of wind chimes—punctuated her question, then there was a flurry of bright silk and a glimpse of a delicate slipper before Hannah herself appeared on the landing.

Delaney's stomach clenched when he saw that she wasn't dressed yet, but wearing a gayly flowered wrapper that clung to every natural curve of her, and her hair wasn't done up yet in its customary auburn knot. Instead it fell in a cascade of damp curls over her shoulders and bodice. She stood dabbing at those curls, almost caressing them with a small towel while sunlight through the stained glass window decked her from lovely head to dainty toe in rubies and sapphires and emeralds.

"Abel, what...?"

Even as she spoke her gaze latched on Delaney at the foot of the stairs. "Sheriff?"

Their eyes locked, and—as always—Delaney could feel his stomach tighten again when he perceived the quick jolt of desire in Hannah Dancer's expression. Then, just as quickly, the desire was replaced by a different sort of recognition. In rapid succession came blinking bafflement and finally white, wide-eyed fear.

She knew, Delaney thought. Not a word had been spoken, but somehow she knew!

The towel fell from her hand as Hannah wobbled and reached out blindly for the bannister. Delaney propped his shotgun against the wall and took the flight of stairs in three long strides to keep her from tumbling down. Hannah sagged in his arms like a doll stitched in silk and stuffed with the downiest of feathers.

By now the schoolteacher and the banker had abandoned their breakfast and were standing, wide-eyed as well, in the vestibule with Abel Fairfax.

"Good Heavens! Mrs. Dancer's fainted," the young woman cried.

"I'll go get Doctor Soames," the banker quickly volunteered, and he was out the door before anybody could say it probably wasn't necessary, and the door had hardly closed behind him before the plump little schoolteacher rucked up her skirts and came charging up the stairs.

"Thank heaven you were here, Sheriff Delaney," she said. "My stars! Mrs. Dancer might have fallen and broken her poor neck, otherwise."

If it weren't for him, Delaney thought, and whatever she had witnessed in his expression, Hannah wouldn't have fainted in the first place. "Maybe you could show me where I might put her down, ma'am."

"Down the hall and to the left," Abel Fairfax called. "You go ahead and show him to Hannah's room, Miss Green."

"Yes. All right. Sheriff, if you'll just follow me."

She bustled ahead of Delaney, until farther down the hallway, she opened a door. "In here," she said. "You can put her on the bed."

Delaney angled Hannah Dancer's lax body through

the doorway and lowered her gently onto the huge carved walnut bed that dominated the room.

Miss Green produced a linen hanky, moistened it in the washbowl, and began to smooth it across Hannah's forehead, crooning a little and murmuring soft words of comfort.

Feeling helpless at best, Delaney just stood there. Rather than stare at Hannah's fragile form on the bed, he let his gaze wander around the room. Her room, to all appearances. Hers alone. There wasn't a single masculine touch he could discern. Not a pipe rack or an errant boot or so much as a cuff link on the dresser.

Instead there were silver hairbrushes, delicate tortoise combs, perfume bottles that captured the sunlight in prisms and sent it spilling across the carpet and over stray garments of cream-colored silk tossed here and there. The lamps were painted with roses to match the paper on the wall. The whole room, in fact, smelled like a rose garden. Lush and sweet and... Well, pink. No, not pink. It was richer than that. It smelled rose. A rich, deep and full-bodied rose.

The door to the wardrobe stood slightly ajar, and Delaney could see yard upon yard of fine silks and serges. He saw an inch or two of green plaid and recognized it as the dress Hannah had worn the evening he'd met her at the lemonade social. He remembered how the deep green garment had set off her eyes and how the gloss of her red hair had rivalled the shine of the taffeta.

And then he'd been introduced to her husband.

Ezra had shaken his hand with great gusto, and Delaney had hardly looked at Hannah again. Until now.

God almighty. He had no business here in her room, he told himself, then strode to the door, down the hall and down the stairs without looking back. If Doc Soames hadn't been coming through the front door just then, Delaney would've been gone.

"What's this I hear about Ezra?" the elderly doctor asked. "Dead by his own hand?"

"It looks that way," Delaney said.

Abel Fairfax joined them. "He took a turn for the worse yesterday, Doc. You know how sick he was. I expect Ezra wanted to go on his own terms, not wait till he was too weak to open his eyes much less pull a trigger."

The doctor nodded somberly. "And Hannah? Have you told her yet?"

"She knows," Delaney said.

"Fainted dead away," Abel added. "She's upstairs, lying down."

"Well, in my experience it's best to put a goodly amount of sleep between bad news and reckoning with it." The doctor patted his black bag. "I'll just go on up and give her enough laudanum to let her get a healing rest."

Delaney almost stopped him. In his opinion, facing tragedy was far better than sleeping through it. He sensed that Hannah would agree. But then it wasn't for him to say, was it?

"Well, I guess that's that," he said. "I'll be getting back to the office now."

"Thanks for your help, Sheriff," Abel said. "I'll be sure and let Hannah know."

"That's not necessary, Abel. You just give her my sympathies, will you?"

"I'll do that, Delaney. I'll surely do that."

The undertaker's buckboard rattled past Delaney as he walked back to the sheriff's office. Ezra Dancer's body lay in back, covered by a dark wool blanket.

"Durn shame," Seth Moran called down from the wagon seat as he passed.

"Yep."

There wasn't anything more to say, so Delaney veered left, out of the cloud of dust the undertaker kicked up. Once inside his office, he aimed his hat at the hook on the wall and propped his shotgun against the desk before he settled in his chair. It felt like noon, but it was barely nine o'clock. Death did that, he mused. Made time feel different. Slowed it down. Speeded it up. He wasn't sure which.

In the war, some battles seemed as if they were going on for several days when in fact they only lasted from dawn until dusk. Others, when they were over and the casualties counted, seemed to have taken place in the blink of an eye.

Hell, it seemed like months ago that Ezra Dancer had dropped by the jailhouse, poured himself a cup of coffee, and sat just to chew the fat with Delaney, to ask him how he liked Newton after his six-month stint as sheriff, if he meant to stay or if he thought he'd be pulling up stakes once his year's contract ran out. But that visit had taken place a mere two or three weeks ago. And Ezra hadn't even struck him as all that thin or ill.

Now the man was dead by his own hand. Delaney closed his eyes a minute, refusing to entertain any thought of what he might have missed in the man's conversation or an expression of hopelessness he might have failed to recognize on the older man's face.

The truth was that Ezra had seemed just fine to him. He wasn't a damned mind reader, after all, and he'd been directly responsible for enough deaths himself over the years to know that in this case he wasn't to blame at all, either for what he did or failed to do.

Sick or not, Ezra Dancer struck Delaney as nothing but a damn fool to leave a woman like Hannah a minute, a single second, a mere blink, before he absolutely had to.

Chapter Two

Hannah wasn't sure if she was alive or dead. Sometimes it felt as if she were deep underwater, struggling against strong currents, not drowning so much as already drowned, breathing water now rather than air. Then sometimes it felt as if she were soaring, lighter than air itself, invisible as wind.

Sometimes she thought that she was in her bed because she recognized the smell of sunshine in the linen sheets and felt the familiar caress of her favorite pillow, the way it tucked so perfectly between her shoulder and her chin.

Her bed, perhaps, yet every time she attempted to open her eyes, her room seemed different. It kept changing. Once the curtains were open and there was sunlight on the elm outside her window. Then it turned somehow to moonlight. And then the curtains were drawn tight, and the only light was the pale flicker from the lamp on the nightstand.

There was always someone in the rocking chair

across the room. Once it was Miss Green. Hannah saw her clearly. Once it was Abel Fairfax. For a moment it seemed to be Ezra.

Ezra. Something about Ezra.

Then she envisioned Delaney, tall and somber at the foot of the stairs. His arms were going around her and she could feel the rough touch of his wool vest and all the warmth beneath it. There was the sudden scrape of his cheek against hers.

Hannah tried to speak, but she was under water again and the current was stronger than before, pulling her down relentlessly.

"There," whispered Miss Green. "There, there. Just sleep now, you poor dear. You'll feel ever so much better in the morning."

Two days later, sitting beside Ezra's casket in the darkly draped front parlor of the Moran Brothers' Funerary Establishment, Hannah had to remind herself once again that Ezra was no longer in pain. She'd watched the cancer eating away at him, dulling the light in his eyes, creasing his forehead, and weighing down the corners of his mouth, especially when he thought she wasn't looking.

But now he had freed himself of all that agony, hadn't he? Rather than allow his illness to waste him away over the course of the next few months, Ezra had mastered his own fate. He had mastered his own death. Above all else, he had vanquished the terrible pain. That alone should have given her great consolation.

Hannah edged a hand beneath the folds of her black veil to wipe away one more tear.

How like Ezra to take fate in hand. His suicide shouldn't have surprised her. She should have been prepared. She should have read it on his face the night before he shot himself or tasted goodbye on his lips when he kissed her good-night.

Or perhaps somewhere deep inside she had suspected Ezra's intentions, yet had chosen to deny if not completely ignore her knowledge. Life without Ezra, after all, was unthinkable. They'd been together fourteen years, half of Hannah's life.

"Mrs. Dancer, please accept my deepest sympathies on your loss. If there's anything I can do for you—anything at all—you only have to say so."

Through her veil, Hannah recognized the brown checkered suit and polished brogans of Henry Allen, the young banker who'd been boarding at her house for the past year. She hadn't seen Henry since Ezra's death, having kept to her room until the house was quiet and all the boarders were asleep. Now the young man stood gazing at her with his brown puppy eyes. If he'd had a tail, Hannah thought, he'd be wagging it. Instead he was dragging the brim of his bowler hat through his fingers while he rocked back and forth in his glossy shoes.

"Thank you, Henry. It was kind of you to come. Ezra would be very glad and grateful."

His puppy eyes grew darker, more glossy. His voice lowered to the intimacy of a whisper. "Shall I wait and see you safely home?"

The boy's sweet on you, Hannah. Suddenly she heard Ezra's voice as clearly as if he were standing right behind her, chuckling as he always did whenever Henry Allen said something particularly syrupy, or something punctuated by undisguised sighs.

Can't say I blame him, either. You're a fine-looking woman, Hannah Dancer. You don't see it in yourself, honey, but others surely do.

A chill edged along her spine, and Hannah sat up a little straighter. "Thank you, Henry. I expect to be here quite a while until everyone's paid their respects." She looked across the parlor where her other boarder, Florence Green, sat with a teacup and saucer balanced on her knee. "Miss Green's been here a long time. She looks a bit tired to me. You might offer to see her home, Henry. I'd consider it a favor."

He sighed a rather boyish, recalcitrant sigh.

"I'd appreciate it enormously," Hannah urged. "Oh, and you might leave a light burning in the vestibule for me, too. I believe I forgot to do that earlier."

"Are you quite sure I can't…?"

"No, thank you, Henry."

Hannah let out a small sigh of her own when he walked away, and was heartened, even relieved, when the young man approached Miss Green and apparently offered to escort her home. The plump schoolteacher put aside her teacup, then rose and took Henry's arm quite somberly. Then, after a last lingering glance toward Hannah, the young man escorted his companion out the door.

People came and went during the next few hours. People who were sorry, shocked, saddened, oh so sad. By ten o'clock Hannah was nearly numb and thankful, not only that her veil hid her reddened eyes, but that it disguised an inappropriate yawn or two. She hadn't had a good sleep since she woke from her laudanum-induced stupor two days ago. When the final mourner shook her hand and murmured his sympathies, Hannah was eager to get home, to take off her black bonnet, her black dress and stockings and shoes, and to fall into a deep and unworried sleep.

"Looks like that's it, Miz Dancer." One of the Moran brothers—Hannah wasn't sure if it was Seth or Samuel—plucked his watch from his pocket and clicked it open. "Ten o'clock. Pretty late. Your husband had a lot of friends."

"Yes, he did." Hannah wasn't sure what to do or say next. She'd never had to preside in a funeral parlor before.

"I'll send a boy around tomorrow with all these flowers," Moran said, gesturing toward the many vases that decorated the room. "Just let me lock up and I'll see you home."

"That won't be necessary, Mr. Moran. It's only a little way. I'll be safe enough."

"You sure?"

"Yes, I'm very sure. After such a throng of people, I think I'd prefer being alone for a while. Will you be picking me up tomorrow for the ride to the cemetery?"

"Yes, ma'am. Nine o'clock, if that suits you."

"Nine will be fine. Thank you, Mr. Moran. Thank you for everything. I'll see you then."

Hannah took a last look at the closed casket and felt her tears welling up again. Ezra was dead. The notion kept surprising her somehow. The hurt kept feeling fresh. Raw. She wondered how long it would be before she truly accepted the fact that Ezra was gone, that she was alone.

A soft breeze riffled her black satin skirt and bonnet when she stepped outside onto the planked sidewalk. The night was warm. She breathed deeply, cleansing herself of the smell of funeral bouquets and the lingering camphor and cedar that scented the mourners' best clothes.

Beyond the brass carriage lights that flanked the Moran Brothers' doorway, Newton was bathed in silver moonlight. Even the dirt of Main Street glistened here and there where moonbeams pooled. Down the street, Hannah could see the elm-shadowed facade of her own house. There was a lamp burning in the vestibule, turning the stained-glass fanlight over the door to glittering jewels.

For a moment everything was beautiful, almost magical. Then Hannah remembered Ezra was dead, and the beauty of the night seemed to mock her. Everything silver suddenly seemed to tarnish. A feeling of such loneliness engulfed her that she had to reach out to the hitching rail to steady her liquid knees.

"Kinda late for a lady to be walking home alone."

Delaney's voice—its deep, rough music—came out of the darkness. Hannah would have known it anywhere. Out of the corner of her eye, she saw the glint of moonlight on the badge pinned to his black vest and the dull sheen of his ever-present shotgun.

"I'm sorry about Ezra, Mrs. Dancer."

"Thank you, Sheriff." Hannah stepped off the sidewalk, into the street. Without asking permission, Delaney fell into step beside her, so close at first that their sleeves brushed, causing both of them to veer slightly—Delaney to his right, Hannah to her left— leaving a foot or so of moonlit road between them.

"I understand you were the one who kept me from pitching down the stairs the other day. I'm very grateful, Sheriff."

"It was nothing," he said, his gaze directed straight ahead. "Glad I was there to help."

They walked in silence then. Well, not total silence. There was the clash of piano music coming from several saloons behind them, a bright peal of laughter drifting out a window somewhere, and a chorus of crickets on the edge of town. Hannah's satin skirts rustled softly while Delaney's spurs kept up a gentle, metallic beat.

When they passed the jailhouse, Hannah caught sight of the chair where this man usually sat, shotgun at hand, casually keeping watch over the town. It seemed odd to stare so boldly at that chair now. Ordinarily, when she walked into town, she riveted her gaze on the opposite side of the street. The sight of him forever flustered her.

They were halfway up the flagstone sidewalk to her house when Delaney halted.

"I'll wait till you're safe inside."

For a moment Hannah wanted to stop, too, rather than continue, alone, toward the huge house. It was happening again—that magnetic pull she always felt whenever she was near this man. She'd been intensely aware of it from their very first meeting last winter. At the first, surprising sound of his well-deep voice and the sight of his serious face with those frank hazel eyes, Hannah's heart had quickened inside her.

Then, after the lemonade social to welcome the new sheriff to Newton, there had been the Valentine's Day dance and a similar tug at her heartstrings seeing Delaney across a crowded room. It had confused her in the past, even irritated her, but now it shamed her—feeling that same pull—with Ezra just a few days dead.

"Good night, Delaney." She said it almost stiffly as she forced herself to walk the final yards to the front steps, and then up to the door. With her hand on the knob, Hannah was tempted to turn and take one last look at the tall man in his black vest, black trousers, and boots. She feared, though, that if she did, she might turn to a pillar of salt.

So she went inside and softly closed the door behind her.

Delaney didn't go back to his room at the National Hotel. Instead he pushed through the doors of the Longhorn Saloon and settled himself at a table in the back. In a matter of minutes, Ria Flowers had brought him a tall, wet glass of beer and had planted her bountiful self in the chair next to his.

"I haven't seen you for over a week, Delaney, darlin'. Don't tell me you're loving up some other girl." She leaned forward, a seductive smile on her red-glossed lips and a significant amount of cleavage shimmering above her crimson laced corset.

Delaney found himself oddly and uncharacteristically immune. Ria was a beautiful young woman still on the spring side of twenty, blond and blue-eyed and finely constructed even without the unnatural allure of her tight-laced corset. Of all the women who made their livings in the saloons of Newton, she still had a softness about her, not the sulky demeanor of most whores.

It had become Delaney's habit over the last several years, as he went from one wild town to another in Kansas, to take his pleasures in each place with just one woman. So, there'd been Joy in Abilene, Josette in Wichita, Fanny McKay in Dodge, and now pretty young Ria Flowers in Newton. It was a sort of monogamy, he thought, unsanctified as it was, unholy perhaps, but ultimately a necessity Delaney could not deny or do without.

Besides, since he never intended to get married again, it wouldn't have done to get cozy with a proper single lady who had…well…expectations. Not that it was always easy walking away from a whore he'd had an affection for, but it was legal. Unlike Wyatt and Doc, he'd never lived as man and wife with such a woman.

In Delaney's view, his two friends might just as well have been married to their paramours for all the grief they cost one another. He'd seen Mattie crying more than once over Wyatt. And if Doc's Kate never shed a tear, still he thought he could read chapter and verse of sadness in her eyes.

"You tired of me?" Ria asked him now, her pink tongue glossing over her lips and her fingers smoothing up and down his arm.

"Just tired, honey." Delaney took a long draft of the warm beer in front of him, then set it down again. "It's got nothing to do with you."

It had to do, he thought, with a red-haired widow whose face and form seemed to have taken up permanent residence in his mind these last few days. The smart thing to do now, he knew, would be to take Ria upstairs to bed, to lose himself if only for a night in her arms and her giving flesh. That was, after all, why he'd come to the Longhorn instead of returning to his room.

But he didn't feel particularly smart at the moment,

and somehow being with Ria Flowers didn't seem like such a good way to rid his mind of Hannah Dancer. It struck him as dishonest. Damned if he'd ever coupled honesty and lovemaking in the same breath. And damned if he'd ever turned his back on a warm and willing female.

He drained his glass and set it on the table with a thump. "I think I'll just turn in for the night," he told her.

"Well, if that's what you want." Ria's lower lip slid out. Worry flickered in her eyes. "I could come with you to the hotel, Delaney. Harry wouldn't mind." She angled her head toward the bartender. "Here. There. It's all the same to him as long as he gets his cut."

He stood up, reached in his pocket for a silver dollar, and pressed it into her hand. "Harry doesn't need to take a chunk of this, honey. You keep it. I'll see you later. Tomorrow maybe."

"You sure?"

"I'm sure." He bent to kiss her forehead, then caught a whiff of her orange-blossom talc and nearly changed his mind. Nearly. "Good night, Ria."

His room on the second floor of the National Hotel was similar to all the other hotel rooms where he'd resided during the past decade of lawing. This one had new wallpaper, though, unlike the fly-specked patterns of some of his former residences. The mattress was decent enough and there were fresh sheets every two weeks.

He propped his shotgun against the wall between the nightstand and the bed, then took off his clothes without bothering to light the lamp. There was still plenty of moonlight coming through the window to keep him from cracking a shin on the rocker or tripping over the worn Oriental runner.

Delaney dropped onto the bed. It was true, what he'd told Ria. He *was* tired. God, he was tired. Of his present circumstances. Of Newton. Of living in this hotel. Of a job that paid him just enough to keep on being poor.

Out of habit, he flexed his right hand—the hand that had once been fast and deadly accurate. That hadn't been the case since he'd been shot last summer in Dodge by a fool kid who wanted to earn a reputation by killing an Earp. But the boy had winged Delaney instead, then found himself pistol-whipped by Wyatt and Virgil both and promptly tried and sent to jail. If it hadn't been for the kid's bad aim, Delaney would probably be in Arizona now.

He'd come to Newton last winter less by choice than by default. With his gun hand out of commission, he knew he couldn't pull his weight with the Earps. It was all well and good that he was still pretty lethal with a shotgun, but then anybody was that. With enough buckshot, even a blind old granny was a threat to life and limb.

Hell, he'd even quit wearing his gunbelt and holster

when he'd come here because he'd felt like a damn fool when he knew they were pure decoration. So he'd locked the leather and iron in the bottom drawer of his new desk, then he'd spent the next couple weeks feeling like a gelding. Just half a man somehow. Not that he thought wearing a gun made somebody a man, but *not* wearing his had taken a definite chunk out of his pride.

He doubled up the pillow behind his head, sighing at the notion that, bone tired as he was, sleep wasn't within easy reach tonight.

Up till now, he'd adjusted pretty well. The shotgun wasn't the total embarrassment it used to be. He'd had the occasional comfort of Ria, and he'd even managed to save a little cash. Not enough yet to buy in with the Earps in all their financial schemes in Tombstone, but enough to at least keep that particular dream alive.

Things hadn't been perfect. Hell, far from it. But Delaney's life had been on a fairly even keel these last few months. Now he felt off center again, detoured if not downright derailed.

Hannah.

He shouldn't have walked her home tonight. He should have just stood there, out of sight, and watched to make sure she got to her door safe and sound. But something always drew him to her like a magnet, like a dizzy moth to a dancing flame. Whatever it was, Delaney didn't care for it one bit.

It was time to start thinking about leaving town.

So what if he couldn't grip a pistol anymore? Doc Holliday did well enough with his sawed-off shotgun and nobody thought any less of him. So what if Delaney couldn't buy into a silver mine or a saloon right away? He could save money in Tombstone just as readily as here. Maybe more, for all he knew.

It was June. There were six months left on his sheriffing contract. He courted sleep by counting the dollars and cents he planned to save before that contract expired.

Chapter Three

It wasn't like Hannah to take to her bed, but that was exactly what she did for the next three days. Right after Ezra's burial, she had joined her little trio of boarders for supper in the dining room, but she hadn't even made it past the soup before she was dabbing her linen napkin at her eyes.

First, Ezra's place at the head of the table—the empty chair and blank stretch of tablecloth—kept drawing Hannah's gaze, again and again. Then Miss Green's continual expressions of sympathy made any other topic of conversation quite impossible. Henry Allen's mournful glances didn't help a bit, and neither did Abel Fairfax's understanding nods or his encouraging smiles.

Hannah had excused herself from the table, rushed upstairs, and hadn't come back down since. The only person she had allowed in her room was Nancy, the hired girl who helped with household chores. Big-boned, raw-knuckled Nancy never spoke more than a word or two and kept her eyes downcast as she came and went with tea and toast or rice pudding. Her silence suited Hannah fine.

She needed that silence and solitude to deal with Ezra's passing, to find her balance now and learn how to be alone after sharing her life with him for fourteen years. Had it really been that long? she wondered. So often it seemed like just yesterday that the big, barrel-chested man in the gray frock coat had come storming into her narrow little crib in Memphis. He'd had a graying beard and mustache back then, but Hannah could've sworn it was gray smoke issuing from his nostrils and mouth.

"Get dressed," he'd ordered her. "I'm taking you out of this foul place."

Hannah had just sat there on the worn mattress, gaping at the huge stranger.

"Come along now. You needn't fear me. Put your dress on and let's go."

When she told him she didn't have a dress, but only the underclothes she wore, he raised his fists toward the ceiling and bellowed like some wounded thing. Then he took off his fine gray coat and wrapped it carefully around her shoulders.

How warm that coat had been. How safe it had felt, shielding her from her chin down past her knees. It had smelled like Ezra, too. Even after all these years Hannah could still remember the pleasant shock of that unique blend of fragrances. One minute she'd been wearing cotton rags, then suddenly she was cloaked in yards of finely tailored wool, in the scents of cherry pipe smoke and rye whiskey and oatmeal shaving soap.

She'd been with Ezra ever since that night in Memphis. There had been at least half a dozen girls her age or younger—all as destitute as they were pretty, most of them orphaned by the war—all of them trading their bodies for a roof over their heads and a pittance of food in their stomachs. Why Ezra had rescued her in particular, Hannah never knew. Somehow she'd never had the courage to ask, perhaps because she was afraid it was all a dream and, if examined too closely, it might simply disappear.

Now, fourteen years later, it was Ezra who had disappeared and Hannah felt more alone than ever before in her life. Part of her wanted to pull the bedcovers over her head and never get up again, but the sensible, strong part of her knew that was a coward's way out. She had a house to run and boarders to tend to. Ezra hadn't brought her to Newton and built this grand mansion just to have them both—Hannah and the house—fall to wrack and ruin after his demise.

Tomorrow, she vowed, she'd rise early, then after her bath she'd don her widow's weeds once more and begin living the rest of her life.

Tomorrow.

She promised.

Just for tonight, though, Hannah pulled the covers over her head once more and wept into her pillow.

* * *

The next morning, when Hannah brought the coffeepot into the dining room, she wasn't surprised to see Abel Fairfax sitting alone at the table.

"I meant to get up earlier," she said as she refilled his cup. "I'm sorry, Abel."

"Nobody minded, Hannah. Henry's gone off to the bank and Florence is down at Galt's Emporium, most likely aggravating the devil out of poor Ted Galt while she hems and haws over stationery and ink." He took a sip of his fresh coffee, eying her over the rim. "You're looking better, Hannah."

She had taken her customary seat at the foot of the table by then and poured her own coffee cup to the brim. "Do you think so, Abel? I feel as if I've aged five years in the past five days."

"It's that black frock. You ought to go back to wearing your regular clothes. Put some color on, my dear. Ezra would be the very first one to tell you that. I'm certain."

Hannah smiled. "He would, wouldn't he? Ezra never much cared for me in black. He was partial to greens and blues."

While Hannah sipped her coffee, Abel finished his oatmeal. Then he dabbed his napkin at his thick gray mustache, folded it carefully, and returned it to its silver napkin ring, which was engraved with an ornate *D* for Dancer.

He leaned back in his chair and flattened his palms on the table. "Hannah," he said. "Ezra left a will."

She blinked, surprised as much by his serious,

rather official tone of voice as she was by his statement.

"I wanted to let you get your bearings before I mentioned it," he added.

"Thank you, Abel. I'm grateful." Hannah wasn't all that sure she had her bearings, but at least it was encouraging that Abel thought so.

She'd always admired him. A widower who'd never had children, he'd come to Newton about the same time Hannah and Ezra had, hoping to start a newspaper in this up-and-coming cattle town. Unfortunately, though, it was the cattle that upped and went after a single wild and newsworthy year. Instead of publishing his own paper then, Abel Fairfax spent most of his time writing letters to the editors of other papers and composing long-winded articles for eastern magazines.

"I studied law back in Ohio," Abel said now. "I don't know if you're aware of that or not."

"You've mentioned it, I'm sure." Hannah noticed now that Abel's brow was even more wrinkled than usual and his lips were pursed thoughtfully, worrisomely, beneath his shaggy mustache. "Is there something wrong, Abel? Something about Ezra's will?"

He didn't answer her directly, but instead said, "Ezra named me his executor. I'd like to read you the will in my office, Hannah. As soon as possible. Not here, though. Do you feel up to walking downtown around three this afternoon?"

Now Hannah frowned. Did she feel up to it? She honestly didn't know. But then she supposed the sooner she attended to legal issues regarding the house—which was, after all, in Ezra's name—the sooner she could get on with her life. Not that it would be all that different from her past, she mused. She'd have the house. She'd have her boarders. Only Ezra's absence would make a difference.

"Three o'clock will be fine, Abel."

"Good." He stood up and headed toward the front door. "I'll see you then." Halfway out the door, he paused. "And don't worry, Hannah. Don't you worry for a single minute."

The screen door closed behind him.

Worry? Hannah thought. Worry? Why, it hadn't even occurred to her.

By three o'clock that afternoon the big June sun had beaten down on Newton for eight straight hours and raised the temperature to ninety-two degrees in the shade. Since they hadn't had rain in several weeks, the unpaved street was dustier than usual.

It was so dusty that Hannah felt like a black broom sweeping toward town in her mourning garb. She wondered how long it would be before the planked sidewalks stretched past the dry goods store, making her walks into town more pleasant not to mention cleaner.

When she lifted her skirt to step onto the sidewalk, several gentlemen tipped their hats and murmured their condolences. Hulda Staub, the wife of the mayor, was exiting the dry goods store just as Hannah passed, and the monumental matron immediately dropped her packages and wound her arms around Hannah, drawing her into a surprisingly tight embrace.

"My dear Mrs. Dancer. How I admire your courage in the face of your loss. How brave of you to be out and about so soon. Lord knows if my Herman passed, I'd barely be able to leave the confines of my bed much less my house."

Caught in Hulda Staub's fleshy embrace, Hannah wasn't exactly sure whether she was being praised or censored. She didn't have time to decide, however, before the heavy-set woman continued.

"Well, now, you must come to our Ladies' Sewing Circle, my dear, on alternate Wednesdays. I insist. We ladies mean to see that you're not lonely."

Hannah had lived in Newton for nine years without ever being invited into this exclusive little group. She had always assumed the ladies disapproved of her because she was so much younger than Ezra and also because, in those early years, she so obviously lacked some of the social polish she had later acquired. Deep in her heart, though, Hannah had a suspicion that these so-called ladies of Newton saw right through her and took her for the working girl she once had been.

She didn't know how to respond to Hulda Staub's invitation. And, to add to her dilemma, Hannah despised sewing and couldn't imagine a worse way of spending her time than convening with a group of matrons, all poking needles through linen while rolling their eyes and wagging their tongues and making soft little tsk-ing sounds.

"Thank you, Mrs. Staub," she said. "It's very kind of you. Perhaps once I'm feeling a bit stronger…"

"Time, my dear," the woman said, seeming to prefer her own voice and opinions to Hannah's. "Time heals all. Shall we expect you next Wednesday?"

"Well, I…"

"Splendid!" Hulda Staub gathered up her packages. "Oh, I nearly forgot to tell you. Mr. Galt just received a lovely bolt of black moire at the emporium. You really must take a look at it."

"Well, I…"

"Good day, my dear."

Before Hannah could reply, the mayor's wife was already bustling away. On her way, Hannah thought, to accost some other unsuspecting citizen. Then she immediately chastised herself for even entertaining such an uncharitable notion. No doubt Mrs. Staub meant well.

But, in the hope of avoiding any other wellmeaning, solicitous folk, Hannah surveyed both sides of Main Street. The few people she saw were minding their own business while doing their best to keep to the shady portion of the sidewalk. Then, although she hadn't planned it, her gaze came to rest on the empty chair in front of the sheriff's office, and her heart promptly fluttered at the sight.

"Oh, Hannah," she muttered under her breath. It wasn't right, that feathery feeling inside her. It hadn't been right when Ezra was alive. It was worse now that he was barely in his grave. It was downright wrong. Perhaps even sinful. Probably so. She ripped her gaze away from that beguiling chair just in time to see Henry Allen bound off the sidewalk in front of the bank.

"Mrs. Dancer," he said breathlessly after sprinting across the street, kicking up dust in his wake. "You shouldn't be out in this infernal heat. Why, you'll melt away for certain."

"I hardly think so, Henry. Unless, of course, you believe I'm made of snow or ice."

His smooth-shaven cheeks flushed. "Oh, no. That would be an insult to one as sweet as you." He crooked his arm in invitation. "May I escort you to Mrs. Tyndall's for a lemonade?"

Instead of feeling flattered by his offer, Hannah was irritated. The silly young man. Why didn't he aim those Cupid's darts and sunbeams at someone who'd truly appreciate them? Florence Green, for example. But Henry appeared to regard the spinster school-teacher—if he regarded her at all—as little more than a fixture in the house, a piece of furniture, a hall clock in the shape of a woman or a table draped in feminine attire.

"Thank you, Henry. That's very kind, but I have an appointment at three o'clock."

It suddenly occurred to Hannah that between Mrs. Staub's aggressive attentions and now Henry's puppyish devotions, she was probably late for her appointment with Abel. Very late.

"Oh, dear. What time is it, Henry?"

He yanked his watch from his vest pocket. "Ten past three," he said.

"Oh, dear." Gathering up her black skirt, Hannah started down the sidewalk toward Abel's office. "If you'll excuse me, Henry, I'm very, very late."

"May I see you to your destination?" he called.

Almost sprinting now herself, Hannah just waved her hand in what she hoped was a polite but firm gesture of refusal.

Being late for the reading of Ezra's will was hardly an auspicious beginning of her new life of independence and responsibility. On the other hand, it struck her as a mere formality. What difference did it make? There was no one else in Ezra's life except her. His parents were long dead, and since he'd been an only child there were no brothers or sisters to be remembered in his will. No long-lost cousins or uncles or aunts. Nary a niece or nephew. As far as Hannah knew, for the past fourteen years, there had been no one in his life but her.

Abel's office was located on the second floor above Hub Watson's saddlery and leather goods. Hannah dragged her heavy black skirts up the outside stairs, all the while dreading being met by deep frown lines on Abel's brow and a disapproving droop to his mustache. She stood on the landing a moment to catch her breath and to steel herself for a possible reprimand for her tardiness, then she knocked on the door, just below the brass plaque that proclaimed "A. Fairfax, Attorney-at-Law, Journalist, Scribe."

"Come in, Hannah." Abel's voice came through the closed door, and she was relieved that he didn't sound unreasonably perturbed or even slightly impatient.

She opened the door and stepped into what could only be described as a dim, dusty maze of books and journals. All four walls were lined with bookcases. More bookcases stood in front of the windows, all but blotting out the light of day. Dozens of bookcases. Crammed bookcases. There were books atop the bookcases, and towers of books on the floor. A veritable librarian's nightmare. What little sunlight that managed somehow to filter through the windows was riddled with motes of dust.

Hannah's skirt brushed against one literary tower and set it to swaying precariously. She was leery of taking one more step for fear of starting a domino effect that would scuttle Abel's entire office in mere moments, so she stood still just inside the door, breathing the musty air and letting her eyes become accustomed to the dim interior.

And that was when she noticed, quite suddenly, that, in addition to all the books, there was a shotgun leaning against a bookcase and, on the far side of the office, someone—Delaney!—was leaning against a window frame.

Abel rose from behind his cluttered desk. "That's all right, Hannah. It's an office, not a china shop. There's nothing that'll break. Here." He chuckled softly as he swept a newspaper off a chair and gestured for her to be seated.

Hannah hesitated. Her heart was in her throat now, getting in the way of speech. "Shall I... Would you prefer if I waited outside until you've finished your business with the sheriff?" she asked.

"No. That won't be necessary. Sit. Come on. Sit right here." Abel glanced over his shoulder. "Sheriff, why don't you take that other chair. Just shove those pamphlets onto the floor."

Delaney's spurs made a soft music when he crossed the room. Then, when he took the chair beside hers, she could have sworn the temperature in Abel's office went up several significant degrees. Out of the corner of her eye, she was intensely aware of Delaney's long legs, even the ropy veins on the backs of his hands and the tanned cords of muscle below his rolled-up sleeves. Before she realized it, she had reached out to grasp a pamphlet on Abel's desk and had begun fanning herself with it.

"I'll make this as quick as I can, Hannah. I know it's uncomfortable in here," Abel said.

Uncomfortable, yes. But it wasn't just the heat, Hannah thought. Why was it she could never breathe properly when Delaney was around? Her chest felt constricted, as if her corset had shrunk a size or two.

"Thank you, Abel." She glanced to her left, tried to mount a tiny smile, then asked, "I suppose the sheriff is here as a witness?"

"Well, no. Not exactly, Hannah. Ezra's will was witnessed a month ago by me and Mayor Staub. Not that Herman knows what's in it. He just signed and certified that Ezra was competent and in his right mind." Abel's gaze moved slowly and deliberately from Hannah to Delaney and back. "Which he was, I think you'll agree, in spite of his pain. Competent, I mean, and in his right mind."

"Of course he was," she said with more than a little starchiness. "Ezra was the sanest man I've ever known."

Delaney merely shrugged.

"All right then." Abel picked up a single folded sheet of paper. "I'll just read this in Ezra's own words. It's pretty simple. No wherefore's or furthermore's or other legal mumbo jumbo. Just his final wishes."

Read it! Hannah wanted to scream. *Let this be done so I can go home. Home where it's cool and I can breathe again.*

After unfolding the paper, Abel stared at it a moment and then began to read. "These are my worldly goods. A house located on the corner of Main and Madison Streets in Newton, Kansas, and all the contents therein. There aren't any secret bank accounts or railroad certificates hidden in drawers or books. There's a thousand dollars in gold, Hannah, and you know where that is. It's yours now.''

Abel peered over the will at Hannah. He raised his eyebrows as if to ask if she understood. Hannah nodded in reply. She knew where the gold was. Over the years Ezra had a habit of stashing coins in the pair of French porcelain ewers on the mantel in the front parlor. Since she was the one who dusted there and had to move the heavy vases, it didn't surprise her a bit that the total came to a thousand dollars.

Abel cleared his throat and continued. ''As for the furniture and all the other contents of the house, they're yours, too, Hannah.''

She nodded again, unsurprised, for she had chosen nearly every stick of furniture and every rug, plate, picture and pillowcase there. ''Fill up our house, honey,'' Ezra had said. And so she had.

To her left now, Hannah was aware of Delaney shifting restlessly in his chair. He seemed as eager to leave as she was.

''About the house,'' Abel read. ''I've given this considerable thought. Delaney, you saved my life last January when my feet went out from under me in front of the bank and the McCarthy boys' wagon just about backed over me. Maybe you don't even recollect what you did.''

Abel glanced toward the sheriff. ''You remember that?'' he asked.

''Sorta.''

Hannah had a vague memory of a bruise on Ezra's arm sometime last winter. It might have been January. "It's nothing," he'd told her. "Slipped on the confounded ice." But he hadn't said a word about any peril or apparent rescue.

Abel read on. "You said it was nothing then, yanking me out of harm's way like that. But it wasn't nothing to me. I was dying anyway, but at least you kept me from dying a cripple or an amputee. I'm grateful to you, Delaney. And so I'm leaving you my house."

Hannah stopped fanning herself. "The house? What was that about the house, Abel?" Surely she hadn't heard him correctly. Surely Ezra hadn't meant...

"That's what Ezra wanted, Hannah. The furniture and everything is yours, but the house goes to Delaney here."

"Why, that's...that's..." She couldn't think of a word to describe her complete bafflement. "It's absurd. It doesn't make any sense."

"Maybe not," Abel said. "But that's the way Ezra wanted it."

The temperature in the office suddenly seemed to increase tenfold, making Hannah feel sick and dizzy. There was some mistake. That was it. Some terrible mix-up. She was certain of that. She'd go home and wait for Abel. He'd explain it then, and they'd laugh at her misunderstanding and everything would be all right.

She stood so fast that she had to grasp the edge of the desk to keep from swooning.

"You all right, Hannah?"

Abel's face became a blur and, when she answered him, her own voice seemed to come from somewhere else if not from someone else.

"Yes, I'm fine. I'm leaving now, Abel. I'm going home."

A little while later Abel Fairfax found himself quite alone in his cluttered office. When he'd finished reading the will, things shook out just about as he'd expected.

Hannah had risen from her chair—stiff as a black umbrella—dazed as a rabbit in torchlight—then steadied herself with a hand on the edge of his desk before heading out the door. She wasn't nearly so careful of his books this time, and sent several stacks toppling.

As for Delaney, he'd sat for a minute, expressionless, like a man whose body had turned to stone. Then, when he'd finally spoken, his voice was closer to a growl than it was to human speech.

"What the hell is this, Fairfax? What the blazing hell?"

In response, Abel had merely shrugged and blinked. Then, like Hannah before him, Delaney sent another dozen books flying as he stormed toward the door and slammed it behind him.

Alone now, Abel stared at the dust motes the man and the woman had churned up in their separate wakes. In the few stray beams of light that managed to pierce his window, those particles were dancing for pure joy.

Abel shook his head and sighed. "I hope you know what you're doing, Ezra, you damn fool."

Chapter Four

What the blazing hell?

Hours after hearing Ezra Dancer's will, it still made about as much sense to Delaney as it had originally. In other words, it made no sense at all.

Sure, he remembered that day when Ezra had slipped on the ice, then couldn't get his feet back under him to get out of the way of that wagon. Delaney just happened to be right there and had done what anybody else would've done by lugging the man out of harm's way.

It had earned him a handshake then and a hearty thanks, and Ezra had mentioned it a time or two later. The man had been grateful. Fine. But gratitude was one thing; a bequest was something entirely different. And a house was...

Judas!

He tilted his chair onto its back legs, eased his head back, then slanted his hat against the bright sunset. It was quiet in town. Just about everybody was home having supper. Those who weren't, but went to the saloons instead to drink their evening meal, hadn't had time enough yet or liquor enough to make any trouble.

If he looked west down the street and squinted against the sunset, he could just make out one corner of the verandah on the Dancer place, nestled in its shady patch of elms.

It was a joke, he told himself again. A man didn't leave a mansion like that to a virtual stranger even if he had saved his life or kept him from breaking some bones. It was ludicrous. Downright crazy, especially when the man had a wife.

No. Delaney told himself he'd heard it all wrong. Maybe it was so dark and dusty in Abel's office that the old fellow had gotten everything upside-down and backwards. He should have stayed and taken a look at the paper himself, but his mind had just gotten scrambled with the shock of it. The widow's, too, he supposed. They'd just about knocked each other over trying to get out the door.

Right now Hannah was probably eating supper with Abel Fairfax and the two of them were laughing at the misunderstanding. Delaney felt his own mouth slide into a grin.

Hell, in all his thirty-five years, he'd never owned much more than a horse and a gun and the clothes on his back. It was a likely bet he never would.

A house! That house! Judas priest. The place had to be worth ten thousand at least. Maybe more. With money like that, Delaney could do a little more than just buy *in* with the Earps. Why, hell. He could buy them *out*.

During supper that evening, Hannah did her best to pretend nothing was wrong. But after Henry excused himself to take his evening constitutional and Miss Green went upstairs to read a new volume of poetry, Hannah couldn't pretend a moment longer. She felt like a teakettle, all boiling and roiling inside.

"Abel, I've been sitting here waiting for you to tell me this is all some terrible mistake," she said. "Ezra's will, I mean."

He shook his head. "It's no mistake, Hannah, although I'll be the first to admit it's, well, unusual."

"Unusual!" Hannah shrieked. "Unusual! Why it's completely absurd, Abel. More than that. It's ridiculous. And it can't possibly be legal."

"Oh, it's legal, all right. A man can leave his property to whoever he chooses." He leaned forward a bit. "Don't you remember reading about that dog in New Haven, Connecticut, whose owner left him a fortune in railroad bonds?"

Hannah rolled her eyes. "Well, at least he knew and treasured the blasted animal. Ezra hardly ever said two words to Delaney that I know of."

"The sheriff earned his gratitude for saving his life, I guess." The older man tucked his napkin under his plate and then pushed his chair back from the table.

"I can't explain it to you, Hannah. I only know what Ezra said in his will."

She'd known Abel Fairfax long enough to know when the man would not be pressed. Right now his mouth was drawn tighter than fence wire, so Hannah kept silent. She wasn't finished, though. She'd have her explanation. Somehow.

In the week that followed, Hannah didn't leave the house. Not once. She sent Nancy, the hired girl, to the grocery store instead of going herself, and she asked Florence Green to return her book to the library and to choose a new one for her. It didn't matter what. Hannah couldn't concentrate enough to read anyway.

Her disbelief at Ezra's will turned first to dismay, and Hannah found herself wandering from room to room in the house she had shared with Ezra for nearly a decade. It was so easy to picture him in his favorite reading chair in the back parlor, or coming through the front door and tossing his hat onto one of the porcelain hooks on the hall tree, or climbing the stairs with his big hand curved around the polished walnut bannister.

She missed him. Dear Lord in heaven, she missed him so very much.

But then her dismay seemed to settle into a profound, piercing anger. And there was, Hannah readily admitted, more than a little self pity, too. How could there not be? How could Ezra have done this to her? How could he have left this house—truly the only home she'd ever known—to somebody else? To Delaney!

And just where was Delaney, anyway? She hadn't seen him since the afternoon Abel had read the dratted will. In the beginning, for a while, she'd entertained the faint hope that the sheriff would knock on the front door, smiling, hat in hand, when he told her it was obvious, just plain as day, that Ezra hadn't been thinking straight and that she shouldn't worry for one second about his taking property that was rightfully hers.

It hadn't happened, though. A week had passed and there had been no word from the man. Not a peep. In this case, Hannah didn't believe for a minute that no news was good news. More than likely, he was probably just waiting for her to do or say something, to make the first generous gesture so he wouldn't appear to be such a greedy, grabby beast. That was obviously his plan. Let Hannah Dancer make the first move. As in *move out* all her worldly goods.

Ha!

Let him wait. Hell would freeze over first.

To say that Delaney spent that week not thinking about the Dancer house wouldn't have been exactly true. He tried not to think about it. Every time the notion cropped up in his brain, he did his damnedest to ignore it. The trouble was that it cropped up so often that trying to ignore it was actually thinking about it.

After he'd considered every angle of the absurdity of the bequest, he got to thinking about what a stroke of good fortune it was. Pure luck. Pure dumb luck. But things like that happened. He knew they did. Why not to him?

Just a few years ago in Abilene a cowhand had been nearly killed in a saloon brawl, then was nursed back to health and happiness by a whore named Ruby Tree. It turned out that he was some rich English duke or earl or something, and—for her nursing skills—Ruby Tree was now the Duchess of Something on Trent.

Things like that happened. Delaney had saved Ezra Dancer's life. That was a fact. Why shouldn't he inherit his house?

So, after *not* thinking about it all week, Delaney found himself knocking on Abel Fairfax's door late one afternoon, determined to resolve this inheritance one way or another.

"I figured I'd be seeing you sometime soon," Abel said, gesturing to a chair littered with papers. "Sit down, Delaney. What's on your mind?"

The sheriff sat, his shotgun balanced across his knees. He cleared his throat. "I don't think you have to be a confounded lawyer or even a genius to figure out what's on my mind, Abel."

"No. I suppose not."

"What the devil was Dancer thinking?"

Abel shrugged. "Who knows? It's not like he

didn't provide for Hannah, you know. The contents of that house are worth plenty.''

"Yeah, but…''

"Plus there's cash,'' Abel added.

"I know that, but…''

"What, then? You feel like you're stealing from the widows' and orphans' fund or something?''

"Maybe.'' Delaney shifted in the chair. "Yeah. I guess I do.''

"Turn it down, then.''

"Don't think I haven't considered it.''

"And?''

"I'm still considering it,'' Delaney said. "I just thought you might have some advice.''

"Talk to Hannah.''

The sheriff blinked. "What do you mean?''

"I mean if your conscience is bothering you so much over this, then talk to Hannah and see if you can't resolve it somehow between the two of you.''

The suggestion, logical as it was, took Delaney completely by surprise. He'd spent so many months avoiding Ezra Dancer's wife that the thought of seeking her out now—intentionally!—for conversation struck him as preposterous. And what the hell would he say to her anyway that wouldn't make him sound even more foolish than he felt?

Sorry about your house, ma'am. But a will's a will, you know. Legal and all that. Plus, a man would have to be a total fool, a stumbling idiot in fact, to turn his back on such good fortune.

"Talk to her," Abel said again.

"All right." Delaney stood up. "I'll do that. I'll do just that. Thanks, Abel."

Someone was knocking on the front door with such force and persistence Hannah was sure the wood was splintering beneath that big fist.

Where the devil was Nancy? she wondered. That dratted girl was never where she was supposed to be. After another series of thunderous bangs, she put her teacup down and went to the door herself. She muttered a curse as she jerked it open.

"Oh."

Delaney was so tall that she found herself staring into the knot of his black silk tie. Her eyes flashed up to his face.

"Sheriff Delaney."

"Mrs. Dancer." He nudged his hat back, then took it off entirely. "We need to talk."

Hannah wasn't sure she could. Her heart was pressing up into her throat the way it always did whenever she was within several feet of this man. She felt her face going up in flames.

"Come in."

Hannah stepped back, and then retreated some more as Delaney crossed the threshold. He stood there a moment, silent, his gaze encompassing the vestibule, and then, with a quick and fluid flick of his arm, he lobbed his black hat onto a porcelain hook on the hall tree.

Hannah stifled a little gasp. The gesture reminded her so much of Ezra. It was so…so…proprietary. No! Not proprietary, she corrected herself. It was presumptive. It was rude and arrogant. This wasn't his home, after all.

Not yet.

Not ever!

"I was just having tea in the back parlor, Sheriff." Hannah turned on her heel, abruptly walking away from him. If he wanted to converse, he could damn well follow her. If not, he could damn well leave.

With her stiff skirts swishing down the hallway, she couldn't hear his footsteps behind her, but when she sat and rather imperiously picked up her cup of tea, Delaney was right there. Close by.

"Have a seat, Sheriff." Hannah gestured rather grandly to a chair. She was, after all, the duchess of this domain, and she intended to remain so. "Would you care for some tea?"

He sat, said nothing. As before in the vestibule, his gaze slowly encompassed the room, and then it settled, frankly, perhaps even boldly, on Hannah.

Her heart quickened. Those eyes—Delaney's eyes—were the most stunning shade of hazel she'd ever seen. An amazing blend of gold and brown and green. Like sunlight dappling elm trees in October. Like autumn itself. The essence of the season. Quite, quite beautiful.

She had to clear her throat before she was able to speak.

"Would you care for a cup of tea, Delaney? Or perhaps you'd prefer coffee? Lemonade?"

She sounded less like a duchess now than a dizzy dolt of a girl, Hannah thought. This wasn't like her at all.

Then, when the sheriff replied, "No, thanks", for a second Hannah wasn't quite sure what it was that he was so politely declining. This was no time to get bumble-brained, for heaven's sake. If there was ever an occasion when she needed to keep her wits—every blasted one of them—about her, it was now.

She remembered then it was tea or coffee or lemonade that Delaney didn't want. Fine. Just what, then, *did* he want?

He leaned forward a little then, his elbows on his knees and a serious, quite sober expression on his face while a keen light played in his lovely, autumn-colored eyes.

"About the house, Mrs. Dancer…"

The house! Hannah stood—snapped to her feet, actually—and at the same time slapped her teacup onto its saucer so hard that the little plate broke in two. The halves landed at Delaney's feet just as he was rising. He had barely stood straight before she lit into him.

"The house! It's mine, Mr. Delaney. And I'll thank you to get out of it. Now."

"If you'll just listen…"

"No. I won't listen. Get out."

"But…"

"Get. Out."

He might as well have been trying to have a conversation with a hornet, Delaney thought. Hannah Dancer was stinging mad and too busy buzzing to listen to a word he had to say. How the hell was he supposed to resolve this business if she wouldn't talk to him? But rather than shout her down, which he felt sorely tempted to do, he decided to take her advice and get out.

"I'll be back," he said.

Her reply was a very undignified snort, which Delaney took to mean that he'd be even less welcome then than he was right now.

In *his* house, goddammit.

Delaney didn't go to the Longhorn that night after he'd made his evening rounds. A few beers and an hour or two with Ria Flowers held little appeal for him now when he needed a clear head to sort out this house business.

"Talk to her," Abel Fairfax had said.

Talk to her. Good God, he'd have to rope her and gag her to do that, he supposed. He'd seen a lot of facets of Hannah Dancer since his arrival in Newton. He'd seen her friendly and polite. Cool and distant. He'd seen her shocked and baffled and sad. But this was the first time he'd seen her mad. What a sight that had been. There was fire in her eyes, a lively blue-green flame, and he swore her hair had turned a deeper, fiery shade of red.

But beautiful as Hannah had been, Delaney didn't particularly want to see that colorful anger again. Not aimed in his direction, that was for sure. And especially when he hadn't done a single thing to deserve it.

Not yet, anyway.

Chapter Five

For the next few days there was enough excitement in Newton that Delaney didn't have time to think about the Dancer house, much less the angry, beautiful woman who resided there.

Seth Akins, who farmed a little piece of land just north of town, apparently dived headfirst into a bottle of whiskey and climbed out drunk as a skunk and meaner than sin. When Mrs. Akins protested, he blackened both of her eyes, then booted her out of their house, locked the doors and windows, and told her he'd shoot their two boys if she tried to get back in.

The woman limped into town, and once Delaney got her calmed down and settled in at Doc Soames's, he headed out to the Akins place alone. Ordinarily he would've deputized a couple of men and broken into the Akins' house in a matter of minutes, subdued the drunk, and been done with it. But with two innocent youngsters held hostage, Delaney decided to do this job alone. He didn't want to chance the misguided heroics of any trigger-happy, grandstanding deputies.

It took him six hours of yelling, arguing, and cajoling through the bolted front door before he convinced Seth to let the little boys go. Then, after seeing that the children got back to their mother all right, it took Delaney an entire night of through-the-door arguing to keep Seth from taking his own life.

If his right hand had been in working order, he could easily have tapped out a window, taken a bead on Seth and shot his weapon out of his hand. But, relegated to his damn shotgun, all Delaney could do was wait the man out. He didn't know which was worse—men trying to kill themselves or him.

Finally, not long after sunrise, the fool succumbed to the effects of too much liquor and too little sleep, and Delaney was able to break through a window and take away Seth's Navy Colt, his old buffalo gun, and Bowie knife.

When he got back to town, with Seth passed out in the back of the Akins' buckboard, Mrs. Akins came flying out of the doctor's office. The woman took one look in the back of the wagon, then screamed at Delaney.

"You killed my Seth. You killed him."

"Now just hold on, Mrs. Akins," Delaney muttered as he climbed down from the driver's seat. "Seth's just—"

She didn't let him finish. The woman called him a bastard, a son of a bitch, and half a dozen other names in a single breath, and then her hand flattened across his cheek with a resounding smack while her foot came down hard on his boot.

The wiry little woman probably would have done a considerable amount of damage if her husband hadn't chosen that particular moment to sit up, inquire as to his whereabouts, and then throw up all over himself and the wagon bed.

"Now look what you've done, Sheriff," the Akins woman snapped, glaring at Delaney before she hitched up her skirts and clambered up into the wagon bed.

"Yes, ma'am." Delaney sighed. "Seth'll be all right once the whiskey's out of his system. If I were you, I'd keep him away from the stuff from now on."

Mrs. Akins sniffed with wifely indignation, then turned her entire attention as well as her sharp tongue on her sick husband.

Delaney should've been used to being unappreciated by now after so many years in this thankless business, but the Akins woman had taken him completely by surprise. He cursed himself for feeling so churlishly disappointed. Then, just as he was turning away from the buckboard, he thought he caught a glimpse of black silk and bright red hair on the far side of the street. His heart seized up for a moment, then settled back with a distinct thump.

Just what he needed right now, Delaney told himself. One more angry female to give him a tongue-lashing, a crack across the face and a kick in the shin, just for good measure.

Well, not today, by God.

He strode back to his office and slammed the door behind him. Hard.

Hannah shrank back against the clapboards of the emporium, trying her best to blend in with the shadows and the dark paint. She had ventured into town, believing Florence Green when the young woman informed her that the sheriff was away, occupied with a disturbance at the Akins farm.

"Imagine the awesome responsibility of talking a person out of committing suicide," the schoolteacher had said before adding a long, warm, and perhaps even infatuated sigh.

Hannah had simply sniffed at that. Awesome responsibility, indeed. Just where was almighty Delaney when her Ezra was putting a pistol to his head? she wanted to ask. Indignant as she was, however, Hannah was happy to hear she would be able to go into town for some notions without having to walk past the steady gaze of those autumn-colored eyes or to chance a confrontation with the man who was trying to take her house away.

She had purchased black silk thread and four yards of black lace at the emporium. She hadn't quite decided yet whether or not to continue wearing her mourning clothes, but if she did, she needed to mend her petticoat. A bolt of green-and-white gabardine caught her eye the minute she walked into the store, and she nearly passed over the black notions for the bright checked fabric.

It didn't seem right, however, putting her mourning aside so soon even though she knew that Ezra wouldn't disapprove. So Hannah paid for the black thread and lace, tucked them in her reticule, and walked outside in time to see Mrs. Akins strike Delaney a vicious blow across the cheek. The sound of the slap seemed to echo all along Main Street.

Hannah's hand flew up to her own cheek as if the blow had landed there. She wanted to cry out or race to the sheriff's aid, but instead she bit her lip and stepped back into the shadows from where she watched Delaney turn his back on the irate woman.

My God, Hannah thought. What man would dare to do what the Akins woman had just done, considering Delaney's reputation? Why, the fool would be lying face down in the street in the blink of an eye, bleeding into the dust. And why the devil would Mrs. Akins strike the man who'd obviously just saved her husband's sorry life?

She watched the tall man stiffen with suppressed anger and then stalk back to his office. She felt the concussion from the slamming door.

Hannah stood there, her breath shallow and her heart fluttering. Delaney was her enemy, wasn't he? He was a threat to her very existence. It didn't make any sense at all—what she was feeling right now— what she was fighting to keep from feeling. Sympathy welled up in her throat, nearly choking her, and it was all Hannah could do not to pick up her skirts, fly across the street, burst through that slammed door, and lay a cool, soft hand to his hot, stinging cheek.

"You must be suffering a sunstroke, Hannah Dancer," she muttered just under her breath, "to even consider setting foot inside the jailhouse. Good Lord! Just go on home. Home. Where you belong."

At supper that evening, the conversation among her boarders kept coming back to the events of the day. Everyone, it seemed, had heard a different version of the Akins affair.

Abel Fairfax and Henry Allen hadn't witnessed the confrontation, but both were certain they had heard that the sheriff had caught Mrs. Akins by the wrist before she delivered the alleged blow. Miss Green had been told by the librarian that the Akins woman had not only slapped Delaney across the face and stomped his foot, but had launched a knee into...well...the region wasn't named, but merely alluded to with a brisk cluck of her tongue and a knowing loft of her eyes.

Hannah, who had witnessed the confrontation, kept silent, doing her best to concentrate on the roast chicken and buttered peas on her plate. But at every reference to that awful slap, she could feel a slight constriction in her throat that had nothing to do with Nancy's overcooked fowl or undercooked vegetables.

It shouldn't have bothered her the way it had—that

shocking blow. Heaven knew she'd been tempted to slap Delaney herself that day he came to discuss the disposition of the house. And if he ever had nerve enough to return, she'd probably have to keep her hands tucked tightly in her pockets in restraint.

Today's incident shouldn't have affected her at all, but Hannah reminded herself she'd have felt the same sympathy for a stricken dog or cat. The tide of emotion that had swept through her meant nothing, really. It wasn't personal. Not in the least. Why, if Delaney had been a lowly beast—and who was to say the man wasn't?—she would have felt a similar, perhaps even a stronger, onrush of compassion.

All of a sudden Hannah realized her dining companions had fallen silent. She looked up from her plate to find them all staring at her rather expectantly.

"Weren't you?" Florence Green asked.

"Pardon me?"

The schoolteacher leaned forward and spoke a little louder now, as if she thought her landlady had gone quite deaf. "I said I believed the incident took place while you were in town. I was wondering if you had witnessed it yourself, Mrs. Dancer."

"No," Hannah said. "No, I didn't."

"Oh. Oh, well." There was a trace of disappointment in Florence's voice and a slight drop of her shoulders, then she turned toward Henry Allen and inquired politely about his day at the bank.

As the conversation continued without her, Hannah chewed a leathery bite of chicken and pushed a few peas around on her plate. She had lied about witnessing the slap. Why on earth had she felt compelled to deceive her boarders about something so seemingly insignificant? She should have said in all honesty, "Yes. I was there, as a matter of fact. I saw the incident, but I really don't care to discuss it."

She could feel warmth begin to spread across her cheeks and tiny prickles of perspiration beneath the bodice and sleeves of her black dress.

"Hannah?"

Abel Fairfax was peering at her oddly now. His gray head was canted slightly, quizzically, and there was the tiniest hint of amusement in his eyes.

"You all right, Hannah?" he asked. "You look a mite peaked."

She felt peaked suddenly. Why had she lied about Delaney? She'd always prided herself on her forthrightness. More than once Ezra had smiled at her and said, "You're a straight shooter, Hannah. I like that."

"It must be the heat, Abel." There was plenty of truth in that. Hannah used her napkin to dab at her moist chin and neck, then folded the linen and tucked it under her plate. "If you'll all excuse me, I believe I'll go upstairs and lie down for a while."

Henry Allen was up from his chair like a jack-in-the-box. "May I be of some assistance, Mrs. Dancer?"

"No, thank you, Henry. Sit down. Finish your supper. Please." *And, please, while you're at it, Henry, turn those soulful eyes and those fond and eager glances upon Miss Green instead of me.*

She fled from the dining room then before the young man could say another word.

Hannah closed the bedroom door behind her, then leaned against it a moment, breathing in the familiar and soothing fragrance of rose petals and cloves in this, her sanctuary. She had chosen a pattern of deep greens and soft pinks for the wallpaper, and the carpet, from Duvalier and Sons in Philadelphia, repeated the same calming hues.

Her agitation immediately subsided. The curtains had been drawn against the harsh late afternoon sun, so she crossed the room now to open them and let in a bit of fresh air. But as soon as she whisked them back, Hannah wished she hadn't.

Delaney was out there, on the opposite side of the street, leaning against the McGuire's hitching post, scrutinizing her house. Hannah immediately shrank back from the window, out of his sight, even though she was certain that he'd already spotted her.

She stood there, hidden in the dusty folds of velvet, not knowing whether to peek outside again or to do her best to ignore the man. What the devil did he think he was doing, anyway? Laying siege to the confounded castle?

She heard the soft but distinct jingle of his spurs then and knew he was crossing the street. Her heart quickened. If he knocked...

...She simply wouldn't be in. That was all. Whoever answered the door could deal with him. She'd be damned...

His footsteps halted just beneath her window. Hannah almost stopped breathing. Her heart was pounding so hard she could hear it. It wouldn't have surprised her if Delaney could hear it, too.

Go away, she wanted to shriek. But instead she just stood there, sheathed in the drapes, hardly breathing, still as a statue, her heart clanging like a bell inside her. *Go away. Go away. Go to blazes.*

The sneeze, when it happened, took her completely by surprise. It didn't even sneak up on her nose, but simply exploded without any warning at all. An unexpected, unfeminine, disgusting detonation. Then another. And another. A veritable salvo of sneezes.

When she finally stopped, there was absolute silence for a moment, then a deep, familiar voice drifted up to her window.

"God bless you."

Hannah clenched her teeth and squeezed her eyes closed, warding off another sneeze. Unsuccessfully. Another volley siezed her.

"Mrs. Dancer? You okay?"

"Yes," she hissed. "Dammit."

"You feel like having that conversation yet?"

"No. Go away, Delaney."

"I'll be back."

"Don't bother."

"Oh, it's no bother, ma'am. None at all."

* * *

The next day it was all Hannah could do not to swat Nancy's ample backside with the cane rug beater after the two of them had wrestled the heavy bedroom drapes to the floor, then lugged them outside and hoisted them over the clothesline.

Hannah took a smack at the green velvet and jumped back when a cloud of dust roiled up. "Why, there's enough dust in these to start our very own desert," she said. "Shame on you, Nancy."

The girl merely glared at her, not a hint of repentance on her face. "Hard getting in to do some people's rooms when them people are always in there."

Hannah sniffed. It was probably true, but she didn't want to hear excuses right now. She just wanted the dratted curtains clean and free of all that confounded dust.

"Here." She thrust the rug beater into the girl's big hand. "Have at it now, and don't you quit till they're clean."

"Yes'm."

Hannah waited until Nancy had taken a few hearty whacks at the velvet, then she turned and headed for the back porch, but halfway there she stopped. Several of the spindles on the porch roof were setting at odd angles. One, no, two were missing.

Her first thought was that she must point this out to Ezra as soon as possible. Her second thought—the one that hit her like a jolt of lightning—was that Ezra was dead. Far beyond telling, or fixing spindles, and well beyond caring what happened to their house. Almost blinded by sudden tears, Hannah stumbled up the porch steps where a loose board snagged the hem of her petticoat and ripped off a good six inches of black lace.

She swore, wrenching loose her skirts and ripping another half a foot of lacy hemline in the process. Hannah swore again. ''Damn blast it!'' And then she banged through the back door, grabbed a hammer and penny nail from a drawer in the kitchen, and banged back out.

Delaney was just coming around the corner of the house, having decided that maybe a back door approach would be less irritating to Ezra's widow. The first thing he saw was the big, rawboned hired girl with a rug beater in her hand. The next thing he saw was Hannah Dancer charging out the back door with a hammer in her fist.

Ordinarily Delaney didn't have all that much of a sense of humor. Things usually struck him as either worrisome or outright dangerous. Rarely in between. Almost never funny. Only now…

Hell, there was hardly a man in Kansas who wasn't afraid of him, yet just yesterday little Mrs. Akins had cracked him a good one across the face and now Hannah Dancer and her slack-jawed helper were about to blast him, too.

''I give up, ladies,'' he said, grinning like a fool as he raised his hands in the air, his shotgun pointed high into the elms.

Nobody grinned back at him, though. The hired girl

grimaced sourly and took another whack at whatever it was she was beating the tar out of. Up on the porch, Hannah Dancer, her red hair flaming in the summer sun and her black skirts whipping in the breeze, glared at Delaney for one fierce and terrible second before she burst into tears.

Chapter Six

He'd never met a man—not one in all of his thirty-five years—who knew what to do with a woman in tears. Hannah Dancer had melted into a pool of black silk on her back porch, and Delaney just stood there, feeling foolish and clumsy and somehow at fault.

It didn't help one bit that the hired girl was looking at him as if it were his fault, or as if he'd just emptied both barrels of his shotgun into the widow and dropped her like a shiny little black bird.

He laid the gun down on the grass and walked slowly toward the porch, thinking all the while that he'd rather be walking down the center of Main Street at midnight toward a trigger-happy drunk than here, in broad daylight, approaching a weeping woman.

"She ain't been right since the old man killed himself," Nancy called before she turned back to beating on the curtains.

Nothing had been right since Ezra Dancer had killed himself, Delaney thought as he mounted the porch steps and squatted down beside the trembling heap of widow's weeds. He could barely see the woman for all the black puffs and pleats. He let out a long sigh, then reached out to touch her.

Don't do it. Not unless you aim to keep her.

The words sounded in his head as if someone had actually spoken them. They were so clear Delaney almost turned around to see if somebody was standing just inside the back door. But he knew nobody was.

Then he stared at his right hand, poised just over the widow's shoulder. The hand that hadn't been right since he'd been shot last year in Dodge and was forced to give up his Colt for the ten-gauge, sawed-off, side-by-side he carried now. A dandy's weapon. Doc Holliday carried one just like it. A grandstander's gun. God almighty, how he hated it.

And as far as his ruined hand was concerned, whatever made him think it could provide a woman like this an ounce of comfort or anything else? Whatever led him to believe he was anything like the way he used to be when he was strong and whole?

A soft curse broke from his lips. The widow lifted her head. Her eyes were wet, green as new leaves after rain, their long, dark lashes all spiked together. For a brief moment, shining that way, those eyes seemed to be welcoming him.

Delaney laid his hand on her shoulder. Gently. Oh, so gently. As if this beautiful woman would break beneath his clumsy touch.

She stiffened instead. Her eyes went dark behind

their gloss of tears, and whatever bright welcome they had offered was gone. He told himself he'd probably just imagined it anyhow.

She swiped the backs of both her hands over her eyes, then jerked up straight.

"You okay, Miz Dancer?" Nancy called.

"Yes, Nancy, I'm just fine." Hannah shot a hot, hard glare at Delaney, then snapped, "Or I will be fine once a certain party removes his hand from my person and himself from my property."

Judas! He'd forgotten his hand was still on her shoulder. It wasn't merely a measure of how this woman dazed and distracted him, but of just how much sensation he'd lost in his bad arm.

"Let go of me," she shrieked. "Get away."

She grabbed for her hammer just as he was removing that errant hand, and the next thing he knew his fingers were curled around her wrist, tightening as hard as he could to keep her from cracking his skull.

But not nearly tight enough! His grip wasn't much stronger than a baby's puny fist. He knew that immediately even though she didn't pull away. She could have, though, and she knew it. Didn't she just know it!

Delaney could see that sudden knowledge in her eyes, like a hot white bolt of lightning. Hannah Dancer seemed to know she had won something in that instant—Delaney didn't know what—and she seemed to be as dismayed by her mysterious victory as he was.

She blinked, letting go of the hammer. It hit the porch boards with a dull thump. Delaney's fingers loosened on her wrist, but didn't release her. Her bones were so delicate. Porcelain, he thought. Her flesh was smooth as satin and warm as the summer itself. He felt her pulse quicken beneath his thumb. Good God, at least he could still feel and appreciate that.

How long they remained that way he couldn't have said. It seemed like a long time. An eternity. A thousand, maybe a million hard beats of his heart, before he was distracted by a cough.

Nancy, the hired girl, stood looming over them. "I said I'm done with them curtains, Miz Dancer. If there's one speck of dust left in them after all that swatting, I'm durned."

It was as good a way as any, Delaney figured, to break whatever spell they'd been under. He released his feeble grasp on Hannah's wrist at the exact moment that she pulled away.

He levered to his feet and, with his good hand, helped the widow to hers before she could protest. Then he bent and retrieved her hammer.

"You dropped this," he said, as if she'd only done it a second or so before, as if nothing else had happened between them, as if his heart had begun to settle back to its normal pace.

She took the hammer from him just as casually and pretended as if she didn't hear the little hitch in her breath when she thanked him.

"It was nothing, ma'am," he said, heading down the porch steps, wishing it had been nothing, knowing it had been something, wondering what it was.

Delaney got drunk that night. Stinking, stupid drunk.

Since it wasn't his habit to have more than one or two shots of whiskey in public, he bought a bottle at the Longhorn and took it back to his room at the National Hotel.

"Want to bring that up to my room?" Ria Flowers had asked him just as he was sliding his money across the wet bartop.

"Not tonight."

There must've been a look about him then—dangerous, perhaps even demented—because Ria hadn't argued or even tried to coax him to change his mind. Well-practiced in hiding disappointment, she gave her bare shoulders a little shrug and sashayed back to her usual seat at the faro table.

On his way to the hotel, the whiskey bottle tucked under his arm, Delaney stuck his head in the jailhouse door. His deputy, Lionel Cole, was slung out in the swivel chair, his worn boots up on the desk and a dime novel a few inches from his nose.

"Evenin', boss," he said, looking over the rim of the book. "It's pretty quiet tonight."

"Yeah, it is, Lionel. That's why I'm leaving you in charge. You got any problems with that?"

The young man grinned, swung his feet down and closed his book. "No, sir."

"Good." Delaney started to shut the door, then added, "If I'm not back here by noon tomorrow, you come to the hotel and get me, all right?"

"Sure. All right."

"All right then." Delaney dipped his head toward the bottle and a mournful chuckle escaped from his throat. "You be sure and knock softly, Lionel, you hear?"

The young deputy laughed. "Yes, sir."

Once in his room, Delaney pitched his hat on a slat-back chair and laid his shotgun on the floor beside the bed. He slung himself on the lumpy mattress and scrunched both of his straw pillows under his head. For twenty bucks a month he should have gotten duck down at the very least, but he considered himself lucky to have his sheets changed once every couple weeks.

"Home sweet home," he sighed, lifting the whiskey bottle to his lips, taking the first long pull and letting it slide down his throat like fire along a fuse.

He hadn't bothered with the lamp since there was plenty of street light coming through his open window to see all he needed to see. After another taste from the bottle, his gaze lofted to the rough plaster patch on the ceiling where—or so the story went—a cowboy named Jeeter Finlay had shot off his pistol and killed a traveling salesman in the room directly above.

A lucky shot. Or unlucky from the peddler's point

of view. Delaney scowled and flexed his right hand. He doubted he could even hit the ceiling with his Colt. The two pounds of iron would just wobble in his feeble grasp and, instead of the ceiling, he'd probably wind up shooting himself in the foot.

Well, hell. Then he'd be symmetrical at least with a ruined foot to go along with his ruined hand.

This was the first time in a long time he'd felt the need to lose himself in a bottle. It wasn't self-pity—or so he tried to tell himself—as much as it was the desire to simply forget everything for a while. The only trouble was that his list of things to forget kept growing.

In the beginning, there was just the war and that hellhole, Andersonville. It should have stopped there, but when the Rebs released him, his list lengthened to include his young wife's suicide. The worst part of that—the part that made him feel sick even to this day—was that when he stood at her grave behind the Methodist church in Zander, Illinois, Delaney couldn't picture her face or bring to mind the sound of her voice or conjure up any feeling at all for his departed bride. Caroline Delaney, the headstone proclaimed. 1844-1864. Died for the loss of her love. And *her* love, damn his soul, couldn't even remember what she looked like.

He'd wandered after that, raising hell and drinking way too much in Iowa and Nebraska and Colorado. He'd work—shooting buffalo, driving wagons, riding shotgun, it didn't matter—till he had enough money not to work, and he kept up that sorry cycle until he'd met up with the Earps in Kansas and they convinced him to put his talents with a sidearm to civic use.

Still, he wasn't family. And now Wyatt and Virgil and Morgan and all their women were trying their combined luck in Arizona, and Delaney was here in Newton, in a sparsely furnished hotel room, alone, toting up his losses and looking for solace in a bottle.

As if the Earps would care if he showed up in Tombstone using a bow and arrow or a damn sling-shot. The bullet that had ruined his gun hand had been meant for Morgan. All the brothers were grateful, sympathetic even, but that didn't change the fact that Delaney—who used to be faster and far more accurate—no longer regarded himself as their equal. Equal! Hell. A blind, arthritic grandmother could be as good with a shotgun as he was now.

If only…

He put the bottle on the nightstand, then levered up from the bed. For a second his head swam and the floor seemed more like water than pine wood, but after a few deep breaths he felt almost sober. Sober enough to locate his Colt Peacemaker nestled in its holster in the bottom bureau drawer.

The heft of it was so familiar. Its solid weight seemed like a part of his own body after wearing the weapon for so many years. Delaney straightened up and put the gun belt on, letting it ride low on his hips the way he always had. The buckle's shaft slid easily through the well-worn leather and he cinched it tight, thinking maybe his hand had improved some. Either that or buckling a belt was such a natural task that even numb, liquored-up fingers could still go through the motions well enough.

It felt good, wearing the gun. Delaney felt balanced again. Centered. Stronger. Whole. Without having to tote the shotgun, his hands were blessedly free.

He'd stashed it away months ago when practicing his draw turned out to be as much a waste of time as it was depressing. Now he lifted the gun an inch or so in the holster, testing it, testing himself. The leather had dried out considerably and the pull was rough, not smooth as it had to be to survive in his line of work.

He dropped the pistol back, flexed his hand, then went for it again. This time not only did he clear leather, but his left hand—the good one—automatically fanned the hammer and his right index finger— the one that shouldn't have worked—twitched hard on the trigger. The Colt exploded in Delaney's grip. At the same instant, on top of the washstand, the pitcher broke into bits and the mirror just above it shattered.

Delaney let go of an oath almost as loud as the report of the gun. What a fool thing to do. He must've been crazy or a lot drunker than he'd imagined not to have checked to see if there was a cartridge in the chamber.

It didn't even take two minutes then for the knock on his door.

"Everything all right in there, Sheriff?"

He recognized the voice of Howard Spence, the owner and night manager of the National Hotel. He could almost picture the wiry, bespectacled man on the other side of the door with Alma, his two-hundred-pound wife, looming behind him in her horse blanket of a bathrobe.

"Everything's fine," Delaney called. "My gun went off while I was cleaning it."

"All right then," Spence muttered.

"Ask him what got broke, Howard."

"Aw, hell, Alma..."

"Go on. Ask him."

Delaney could almost hear the woman's elbow spiking hard into her husband's rib cage.

"Uh. Anything broken in there?" the man asked.

"Nothing I can't make right," Delaney replied. "You can add it to my next month's rent."

"You bet we will," the woman said. "Howard, you tell him that rent's going up, too. I won't have anybody shooting up my place. You tell him."

"Hush up, Alma."

"Tell him!"

Howard Spence cleared his throat. "Uh, Delaney...?"

"I heard."

Delaney heard the same threat the next morning while he was making his way through half-dead potted palms and across the threadbare Oriental carpet in the hotel's lobby. After draining the whiskey bottle the previous night, tossing and turning and feeling his room doing the same, then waking up with a headache the size of a Halloween pumpkin, he was in no mood for big, loud Alma Spence.

"You might be the law here, Sheriff," she called, "but that don't mean you don't have to pay for what you break. You hear?"

The way her voice boomed across the lobby, he was pretty sure half the town heard her. For a second, Delaney was sorely tempted to raise his shotgun and blast her where she stood behind the desk. Lord knew she was a tempting target, big as the broadside of a privy and twice as ugly.

Fine thing, he told himself, letting a female get his goat this way, allowing Mrs. Spence to nudge his temper to its limit. There'd been a time her yammering wouldn't have bothered him any more than a gnat.

He'd lost a lot more in the past year, he feared, than the ability to use a six-gun. He'd lost his center, that quiet and untouchable place that kept him cool in the most harrowing circumstances. He felt less like a man now than a hot-tempered, careless boy. And that, he knew all too well, was a good way to get killed.

"You don't have to put up with that anymore, you know." The voice came from behind him, and when Delaney turned, Abel Fairfax was just lowering his newspaper. "Staying here when you own a whole house just down the street. Doesn't make a lot of sense to me. But I guess you know what you're doing, Sheriff.''

Delaney must've stared at the man like a half-wit then, because Fairfax gave him a smile a person would've bestowed on an idiot.

''What?'' the older man asked. ''It never occurred to you to just move in?''

All Delaney could do was shake his head. He was almost surprised it didn't sound like peas shaking in a tin can. Move in? Hell, no, it never occurred to him. When he thought about the Dancer place, he only thought about selling it. Move in? With Hannah Dancer?

''Of course, I can't promise you Hannah's going to like it,'' Fairfax continued. ''But it's legal. The law's on your side, Delaney. Anyway…'' The older man grinned slyly. ''Who's she going to call? The sheriff?''

Not more than an hour later, Delaney stood on the front porch of the Dancer place, shotgun crooked in his left arm and all his worldly goods in the tattered carpetbag by his feet. No sooner had Abel Fairfax mentioned moving in here, than Alma Spence had pounded her big pink fist on the hotel register and bellowed, ''I'll be expecting your next month's rent plus twenty dollars in damages by six o'clock this afternoon, Sheriff. Otherwise your gear will be out in the street at six-oh-five.''

That had torn it, Delaney suspected. Alma's bellowed threat plus the fact that he didn't have the forty dollars she was trying to wring out of him. But he did have a house, dammit. Why not move in?

Legal? Yeah, he guessed it was. To say that Hannah Dancer wouldn't like it was putting it pretty mildly, though, and Delaney wasn't looking forward to tangling with another irate female—a redheaded one, to boot—now that his temper seemed about as dry and brittle as kindling.

He raised his fist to knock on the door, but it whipped open before he even connected with it. There was a little gasp, then a shocked, round face tipped up to his and blue eyes as big as robin's eggs blinked. Delaney recognized the little schoolteacher, but couldn't for the life of him remember her name just then.

"Afternoon, Miss."

She blinked again while her mouth appeared to blink, as well, falling open, snapping closed, then opening again. Plain as she was, she reminded him a little bit of a plump fish just off a hook.

"Oh, my goodness," she said. "Sheriff Delaney! I suppose you're looking for Mrs. Dancer."

Delaney supposed so, too, but he had to admit he was glad the redhead hadn't answered the door herself. If she had, he'd probably be standing here picking splinters out of his teeth after she'd slammed the paneled oak slab in his face.

He leaned his shotgun against his carpetbag and took off his hat. "Is she in?"

"Is she…? Oh. No. No, she's not. I believe she went to the bank a while ago. I have no idea when she'll be back."

Delaney grinned. There was no dragon protecting the castle! No redheaded keeper of the flame. "Mind if I come in?"

The schoolteacher blinked again, then stepped back, as if allowing ample room for the entrance of some not-quite-tame animal.

He gazed around the vestibule with its green brocade wallpaper, its fancy tables and vases, the jewelled light spilling down the stairs from the skylight over the landing. He filled his lungs with the mingled scents of eucalyptus and cloves. *All right, Ezra,* he thought. *You must've had a reason for leaving this place to me, although I'll be damned if I can fathom it. But I'm here now. Damned if I even know why. But I'm here.*

He tightened his grip on his carpetbag. "Maybe you could show me to the empty room upstairs?" he asked the schoolteacher.

"The empty…? Do you mean Mr. Dancer's room?"

He nodded. "I guess that's what I mean. Mind showing me?"

"Well, I…" Her fingers fluttered at the prim lace collar of her dress. "It's just that… Well, you see, I'm not sure…"

The woman reminded him of a porcelain vase—a not very attractive one—wobbling on the edge of a table. In a second or two, she'd be pitching forward and shattering into a thousand pieces.

"Never mind, Miss." He started for the stairs. "I expect I can find it myself."

He found it then, right next door to the room where he'd carried Ezra's widow after she'd fainted last week. And he knew it was Ezra's room immediately because, over the black marble fireplace, was a gilt-framed, nearly life-sized portrait of Hannah.

Delaney stood there a minute, in the doorway, contemplating a retreat. All the way to Arizona, perhaps. He had all his clothes and gear with him. If he turned around, walked to the livery stable and got on his horse, he could be twenty miles away by sunset.

He was tempted to run, by God, even though it struck him as a coward's way out. Still, he had the feeling that once he moved into Ezra Dancer's house, especially into this room where Hannah loomed so lovely over the mantelpiece, his life was going to change.

For better or for worse, Delaney hadn't a clue when he stepped across the polished oak threshold and tossed his carpetbag on Ezra Dancer's bed.

Chapter Seven

Hannah was walking home after depositing Ezra's thousand dollars at the bank, where Henry Allen, the silly fool, had blushed and gushed and practically fallen all over himself assisting her in opening an account. Even so, it hadn't been easy for her, letting go of those gold coins, and she wondered now if they hadn't been safer in their vases on the mantel, where they'd been accumulating over the years.

Banks, after all, could be robbed. That's what Ezra had always said. Heaven knew there were dozens of banks in Kansas that had been in the past few years. Why, only last year a gang of outlaws had tried to rob a savings and loan in Dodge City in broad daylight. Ezra had read her the article in the paper. The only thing that had prevented the men from getting away with nearly seventy thousand dollars in cattlemen's money was the quickness of Wyatt Earp, his brothers, and a deputy named Delaney, who'd been shot during the confrontation.

When Hannah remembered that, she glanced toward the Sheriff's office only to see an empty chair out front. Something twitched inside her, and she couldn't have said whether it was disappointment or relief. Either way, she cursed herself for looking in the first place and then feeling anything at all.

She had stopped feeling much for men in general since those bad days of the war, but particularly since her first day in Memphis when Ben Rathbone had beckoned her into his whorehouse and promised her food and shelter in return for—what was the expression he'd used? Suddenly she could almost hear his whiskey-drenched, cigar-roughened voice as if he were standing right beside her.

I'll take care of you, sis. Trust me. All you've got to do is be nice to my friends. Real nice. You'll get two decent meals a day and a roof over your pretty little head in return for your favors.

Favors. That was the expression Rathbone had used. Hannah, even at thirteen, already knew about those. On her way to Memphis from her burned-out home in Mississippi, she'd been forced to give those favors up to soldiers, both gray and blue. So when Rathbone made his offer, she'd had nothing left to lose and only her survival to gain by accepting.

In retrospect, her months in that house in Memphis hadn't been so terrible. And Rathbone had done as he'd promised, providing two meals a day and a roof over her head. For the most part now, those days and nights in Tennessee were just a blur, a faceless succession of hasty, rough men and the dark-of-night weeping of lonely little girls.

Then Ezra had come and whisked her away to Kansas, and never once referred to that time or those circumstances. It became easier and easier over the years for Hannah to forget it, too. Her life—her *real* life—seemed to have begun with Ezra. Before that—well, she chose to think of that time as only a terrible dream.

She came to a halt in the middle of the sidewalk, staring down the street at her house. For a moment, the house, too, seemed dreamlike, shimmering in the sunlight and the breezy shadows of its surrounding elms. For one heart-clenching moment, Hannah wondered if it wasn't a mirage, if she might awake any second only to find herself fourteen again and back on a thin, straw mattress in her cramped little room in Memphis.

Dear God. Ezra was dead. Gone. Maybe he'd never existed at all. Maybe her good fortune—all of it—had been a dream. Like some fairy-tale waif, she had fallen into a deep and blissful sleep, allowing Ezra to take care of her, sinking into his generosity as if it were a fine feather bed. And now, fourteen years later, she was awake and Ezra was gone and the house he'd built for her—the fairy tale castle— wasn't hers anymore. She was right back where she'd started. The dream was over, and the nightmare of reality had resumed.

Hannah felt as light-headed as a dandelion all of a

sudden, as if a single puff of air might shatter her and scatter her in a million aimless directions. She thought—no, she knew!—she was going to faint. The edges of her vision darkened and her ears began to buzz.

"Mrs. Dancer, are you all right?"

"Hannah, dear. You're looking quite ill."

Hannah heard the women's voices, although at first she couldn't see them. Then she blinked and brought Hulda Staub and Grace Collier, the minister's wife, into view. They were staring at her. Grace Collier reached out and grasped Hannah's elbow firmly.

"Hannah?" she asked again. "Are you ill? You're pale as a bed sheet, dear."

"Yes. No. I...."

With that, buxom Hulda Staub put a hand on each of Hannah's shoulders and pressed her down until she was kneeling in a billow of black silk on the sidewalk. The women's voices—like noisy locusts—continued to swirl and twitter over her head.

"She's probably not eating properly," Hulda said. "Poor little thing."

The minister's wife clucked her tongue in sympathy. "Grief will have its sway, I suppose. How cruel of her husband to leave her this way. Why, I'd be tempted to shoot the cad myself if he weren't already dead."

"I don't know. They say he was ill and in terrible pain," the mayor's wife replied.

"It doesn't matter," Grace said. "Only a coward would—"

"I believe I'm better now." Hannah lifted her head and found that her vision was normal now and the fierce buzzing in her ears was gone, replaced by the women's equally fierce buzz of speculation.

"Here, my dear." Each woman took an arm and assisted Hannah to her feet.

She swayed for a second, then found her balance and took in a deep breath. Better. Yes. She thought so, anyway. "I'm fine now," she said. "Thank you so much for your help."

"There. There." Hulda patted her on the back. "Why you're skin and bones, Hannah Dancer! You must let me bring you some of my lentil and cabbage soup. It has amazing restorative powers. Even the mayor says so, and he's very particular about his diet."

"Hulda is a wonderful cook," the minister's wife chimed in. "Her dishes are the mainstay of our church socials, I must say. I hope to see you at one of those in the near future, Hannah." The little woman wagged a gloved finger. "Sunday morning services would help you carry the burden of your grief. You'd be most welcome."

"Thank you," Hannah replied, wondering if these pillars of Newton society would be quite so welcoming if they knew the sullied details of her past, thinking again how she and Ezra had guarded their secret so well for so long.

Now that secret was hers to keep. And keep it she would, whether or not she kept her house.

Hannah reminded herself again of all the reasons she had avoided forming any close relationships here in Newton. In the first place, she felt inferior to these prim and proper women, most of whom had had far more formal education than she. Why, Grace Collier had even attended a young women's seminary in Massachusetts while Hannah had been lucky to finish fifth grade before the war tore apart her Mississippi county and all its institutions, provincial though they were.

When she was in their company, as now, she was always afraid she would slip and make some reference to her tawdry past. What if they began reminiscing about their school days, or—worse!—what if they recalled their wedding days, or how they first met their husbands?

Hannah preferred saying nothing to being forced to lie, to weave a tangled web that could only trip her up in the end.

"I really should be getting home now," she said. "I'm feeling ever so much better."

"Are you sure?" Grace Collier asked.

"Yes, quite."

"Would you like us to accompany you?"

"No. No, thank you."

"Well, then, we'll be looking for you Sunday, Hannah." Grace patted her arm and smiled sweetly. "I do hope you'll join us at services."

On her way home, with the women waving their hankies and calling farewells behind her, Hannah already knew good and well that she wouldn't be joining them in one of the oaken pews at the Methodist church. Well, she assumed the pews were made of oak. She hadn't been inside a church of any denomination since before her time in Memphis. Not that she didn't feel the need or desire to attend services, but that desire wasn't as strong as her fear of being struck by a lightning bolt as soon as her shadow darkened one of those hallowed doorways.

The Lord, it was said, forgave sinners. Hannah believed that, but she didn't want to tempt His patience or try His forgiveness any more than was absolutely necessary. Perhaps when and if she finally forgave herself, she'd feel comfortable going to church.

Where she was comfortable now was home, so she picked up her skirts and hurried there.

Florence Green was standing in the vestibule when Hannah came through the front door. Or rather than standing, the schoolteacher gave the appearance of hovering, rather like a butterfly that couldn't decide whether or not to land.

Hannah plucked out her hat pin at the same time that she exclaimed, "For heaven's sake, Florence, whatever is the matter?"

"It's him."

"Him?" Hannah frowned.

"He. Him. He's upstairs." Her hand fluttered in the direction of the staircase. "There."

"He who?" Hannah snapped, her patience with the dithering schoolteacher already worn thin.

"The sheriff," she whispered, almost worshipfully.

Hannah, however, didn't whisper in reply, worshipfully or otherwise. She shouted. "Delaney? He's upstairs? In *my* house?"

Florence nodded, much too eagerly in her landlady's opinion. "He came carrying a carpetbag, Mrs. Dancer. I do believe…that is, it seems to me that the sheriff's moving in."

All Hannah could do was stare at the young woman. Her mouth could hardly frame the terrible words. "Moving in?"

"Yes, I believe so." The schoolteacher aimed her moony gaze toward the staircase. "He's been up there for quite a while now." Her whisper turned to mere breath as she added, "In Mr. Dancer's room."

"In…!" Hannah's glare was so hot it could have burned the staircase and turned the carpet to ash. She mouthed an oath that made Florence's wide blue eyes open even wider still.

"We'll just see about that!" Hannah snorted and headed up the stairs, stomping on each tread as if she meant to splinter them all.

She charged down the hallway toward Ezra's room, only to stop abruptly when she discovered the door was closed. Her first instinct then was to double up her fist and pound on the wood panel, but she told herself she'd be damned if she'd knock on a door in her own dratted house, so she gripped the knob, twisted it, and stepped inside.

Whatever threats she'd intended to make or curses she'd planned to scream, all those prickly words stuck in her throat like nettles when she saw the object of her ire stretched out on the bed, sound asleep. Hannah stood there staring, speechless and immobile, telling herself she should turn and leave or at the very least look away, but unable to do either one.

His arms were folded behind his head. His hat was tipped over his eyes, covering his face for the most part, but she could still see a few locks of his dark hair against the white pillowcase. One long leg stretched off the side of the mattress, while the other remained atop the bed, bent slightly at the knee, unable to extend its full length because of the walnut footboard.

Delaney was too tall for Ezra's bed! No sooner had Hannah noticed this than she also noticed that the sheriff had taken off his boots and spurs before putting his feet on the embroidered cotton coverlet. His wool socks were worn pitifully thin at the toes and heels. Why that made her smile she couldn't have said, but she felt her mouth curve upward at the sight.

Her gaze lifted to the portrait over the fireplace. Painted eight years ago when she was twenty, Hannah had never cared for it. Ezra, on the other hand, felt that Karl Pfeiffer, the artist, had captured her perfectly and he had happily handed over the outrageous sum the German had charged, then had hung the portrait prominently in his room.

To this day, Hannah still despised it. It wasn't that she looked ugly. In fact, if anything, Herr Pfeiffer had flattered her by lengthening her neck, slimming her waist and deepening the color of her hair. What she hated about the portrait was that there was something about her expression, something far too worldly, way too knowing. Some curious little glimmer in her eyes. Some almost devilish twist to one corner of her mouth. Something she never could quite pin down, but there nevertheless. Herr Pfeiffer had painted a secret on her face, and Hannah knew all too well what that secret was.

Suddenly she looked back at the man asleep on the bed. Had he dozed off studying her portrait? she wondered. Had he taken note of the secret there? Had he tried to guess the source of the glimmer in her eyes and the faint twist of her lips?

Surely not. Delaney had probably gone to sleep feeling pleased as punch with himself for invading her house while he planned his next move for taking it over completely.

Ha!

He was here now, damn him. Apparently it was legal, so there wasn't much she could do about that. As for the rest…well…Hannah figured anyone with a glimmer in her eyes and a hellion's twist to her lips could give the sheriff a good run for his money.

She was going to keep her house. Hannah didn't doubt that for a single minute.

God almighty! Delaney drew in the first good breath in what seemed like an hour after Hannah Dancer stepped back and closed the bedroom door. For just a second there he thought he understood why Ezra had put a gun to his head and pulled the trigger. The woman was as unpredictable as a tornado and just about as scary.

He'd pulled his boots off and then lain down to rest his whiskey-aching head for a couple of minutes before going back to the office. Instead of resting, though, he'd found himself contemplating the portrait of Hannah Dancer and had barely begun to survey it when he'd heard the woman herself bellowing downstairs and then heard her—skirts whipping and teeth gnashing—come charging down the hallway and then stop and almost rip the knob off the bedroom door.

Rather than confront her—or, coward that he felt, be confronted by her!—he'd quickly shifted his hat over his eyes and pretended to be asleep. It surprised him at first when she didn't throw the nearest heavy object at him and tell him to get himself and his dusty clothes off her husband's bed and out of her house. It surprised him even more when she stood there in the doorway, not saying a word, with her skirts barely rustling and her angry breathing evening out and then, finally, the faintest murmur of pleasure issuing from her throat.

That little sound of pleasure, that soft little purr, had not only confused him all to hell, but it had made him break out in a cold sweat while his blood fairly boiled inside him. Under different circumstances, with a different sort of woman, a soft moan like that meant just one thing and would have driven him nearly wild with desire.

Then she'd retreated and had left him lying there feeling somehow as if a storm had just passed over him, tossed him every which way without even touching him, and disappeared as quickly as it had come.

He moved his head slightly to dislodge the hat that was covering his eyes. Hannah Dancer's portrait stared at him intently. Boldly. Knowingly. If he hadn't known better, Delaney might have thought it was a portrait of some ancient goddess who'd seen everything and done everything—twice.

If he hadn't known better, he might have figured her for a witch who'd cast a spell on Ezra Dancer while he lay in this very bed, and now she was doing the same to him. Or trying to.

A rough sigh broke from his lips. He flexed his right hand, moved his index finger as if it were curled around a trigger. Moving in here had probably been a mistake. No, not probably. It *had* been a mistake. But, if he worked hard and got his hand back to par, he wouldn't be staying here long.

He'd soon have enough cash to buy in with the Earps on an equal footing. That problem had been miraculously solved by Ezra Dancer's will. But financial equality was one thing. Being their equal as a man meant using a sidearm, not some flash-and-splash shotgun. Delaney had waited too long for a miracle in that department. Now he just had to quit waiting and get to work exercising his gun hand.

With six months to go on his contract with the city, and six months of exercising the stiffness out of his muscles and tendons, he was sure he could be on his way to Arizona by Christmas.

Then he took another long look at the bewitching portrait over the fireplace. Cash or no cash. Pistol or shotgun. Riding away from Hannah Dancer was probably the smartest decision he would ever make.

An hour later, while sitting in front of the jailhouse and doing little more than watch the afternoon sun bake the street, Delaney thought about another reason he didn't care to stay in Newton. It wasn't so much the fact that there was little or nothing for a lawman to do, but that the little or nothing that actually did happen got around town with the approximate speed of a ricocheting bullet.

This thought occurred to him while he watched the mayor, Herman Staub, walk out of the bank, tug at the cuffs of his checkered suit coat, and then head down the sidewalk toward the jailhouse with a look that meant business on his beefy face. The man's eyebrows were practically tangled in solemn contemplation.

"Sheriff." The mayor touched the brim of his bowler hat, then dragged a chair up to Delaney's and wedged himself between its oaken arms. "I hear you've moved into the Dancer house."

The big German didn't waste much time, Delaney thought. He merely nodded in reply.

"Taking it over, I hear."

This time Delaney didn't nod, but rather gave a noncommittal little shrug.

"That's a lot of house for a single man," the mayor said. "Are you thinking about selling it?"

"Are you thinking about making me an offer, Staub?"

The mayor rubbed his chin. "Maybe."

The way these things went, Delaney knew it was his turn now to toss out a figure. A sky-high one that would make the German sit back in his chair, shaking his head and muttering *Gott in Himmel.* Then the mayor would lean forward again, his fingers laced together as he casually mentioned a sum that was probably half what he would be willing to come up with when it was all said and done.

It was an old, familiar game. But Delaney didn't feel like playing. Not yet, anyway.

"I haven't made any decisions yet," he said.

The mayor leaned closer. "Well, when you do, I'd appreciate it if you'd let me know first, before you tell anybody else, I mean. My wife fancies the Dancer house." He snorted. "It's all she can talk about these days."

Delaney tried to picture hefty Hulda Staub as mistress there in Hannah's stead. It was a little like replacing a diamond with a lump of coal. Then, as he was imagining that, the diamond herself came into view down the street, walking determinedly in his direction.

"I'd keep quiet about it if I were you," he said.

"What?" Herman Staub followed Delaney's gaze. "Ah. Well, perhaps our discussion is somewhat premature." He stood. "Keep it in mind, though, Sheriff, won't you?"

Delaney tapped a finger against his temple in response, all the while watching the advancing woman. With her quick pace, she was kicking up a little storm of dust around her. The summer sun flamed in her hair. He suspected her temper was equally hot at the moment. If she'd been a man with a gun, he would've had his shotgun levelled on her by now, his finger poised on the trigger.

Mayor Staub, the coward, had already scurried away in the opposite direction when Hannah Dancer's black skirts swayed to a stop just short of Delaney's boots.

He'd be damned if he'd stand like a gentleman and make himself a bigger target, so he simply tilted his hat back and squinted up into her face.

God almighty. For a minute Delaney thought he was looking at her portrait. The expression she wore was exactly the same. Ancient and all-knowing and utterly intriguing.

"I have a proposition for you, Delaney." She

pulled off one glove, then the other, and slapped the soft black leather against her palm. "Are you willing to listen?"

He settled back in his chair, stretching out his legs. "I'm all ears, Mrs. Dancer. As long as you aren't one of those women who just naturally confuse listening with agreeing."

She gave him a withering glance, and then looked up and down both sides of the street before she said, "I wonder if we might go inside your office rather than have half the town attempting to read our lips."

"I expect you're right." Delaney stood and gestured toward the jailhouse door. "After you, ma'am."

Chapter Eight

The minute Hannah stepped into the dim interior of the jailhouse, she regretted it. She was nearly felled by the combined odors of old coffee grounds, tobacco, and gun oil, not to mention what was probably several years' worth of sweat and tears and heaven-knew-what-else that scented the mattresses in the cells.

There were two of those, Hannah noticed. Neither one was occupied, and she felt absurdly grateful for that. At least she wouldn't be humiliating herself in front of the town drunk or a horse thief.

"I've never been in here, you know," she said, turning toward Delaney, hoping he didn't notice the nervous hitch in her voice or the way her fingers were tightened in a sweaty death grip around her gloves. "Here in the jailhouse, I mean."

"Somehow that doesn't surprise me, ma'am." He aimed a small, rather cautious smile in her direction before he settled a wooden armchair on one side of his desk, then walked around and eased into his own swivel chair. The springs creaked when he leaned back, striking a casual pose. "Have a seat, Mrs. Dancer, and let's hear this proposition of yours."

Her proposition. Hannah almost had to shake her head to make her thoughts fall properly into place. Being alone with Delaney hadn't been a good idea at all. She should have requested that he meet with her in Abel Fairfax's office. That would have been altogether proper and businesslike.

But this... This male bastion of metal bars and shotguns and Wanted posters... Her head had felt muddled as soon as she crossed the threshold. It occurred to her that this was really the first time she'd been alone with the sheriff in such close quarters, but she wasn't ready or even willing to concede his effect upon her mental powers much less her senses.

It didn't help matters at all when he crossed his arms, leaned farther back in his chair, and put his feet up on the desk. His boots were well made and well worn, Hannah noticed, but all she could think of were the incipient holes in his socks and how the sight of them had touched her somehow.

She smoothed her gloves out atop her skirt, drying her palms in the process and trying to concentrate on herself rather than Delaney. She had, after all, come here with a specific plan. Her proposition.

"My proposition," she said, "is quite simple, really. I'd be a fool to contest Ezra's will. I've come to accept that, Mr. Delaney." She sighed with soft resignation. "Your moving in today drove that point home quite clearly, I must say. Ezra left the house to you. I don't dispute that, nor your right to live there."

He nodded slowly, then raised his eyebrows as if gesturing for her to continue. If the man felt any surprise or relief or any emotion at all about what she'd already said, he didn't show it. His expression remained…well…inscrutable, as impossible to read as the print on a Chinese newspaper.

"What I feel I need to make clear to you," Hannah continued, "is that my house…" She blinked. "Well…your house, I suppose, isn't just a residence. It's also a business. And, if I do say so myself, a reasonably profitable one."

Hannah paused, ready to answer what she believed was the obvious question. How profitable? She had her figures ready, right down to the last penny.

But Delaney merely continued to stare at her, rocking slightly in his chair, his face still as expressionless as a river stone.

"I have three boarders, as you know, all of whom pay twenty-five dollars a month for room and board. Well, not exactly all. Miss Green pays twenty-two dollars, which I felt was fair, considering that the school board pays her such a pittance."

Delaney's mouth appeared to thin in disapproval, but other than that, he showed no reaction. Perhaps, Hannah thought, he was adding up the figures she'd just presented. If not, she'd do it for him.

"As you can see, that comes to seventy-two dollars

a month. Out of that sum comes grocery expenses, my hired girl's wages, and…''

''What's your point?''

Hannah blinked. ''Excuse me?''

''What's your point, Mrs. Dancer? You said something about a proposition. So far all I've heard is a lot of numbers.''

''Well, I'm getting there.''

How rude! First Hannah had thought he wasn't listening to her at all. Now she knew he'd been listening, but simply didn't give a rat's hindquarters about a single thing she'd said.

''I'm merely trying to make the best of a terrible situation,'' she said, hating that her exasperation sounded so clearly in her voice. Maybe her desperation, too. ''I'm trying to solve our problem.''

''I don't have a problem, Mrs. Dancer.'' His mouth slid into an annoying grin.

''Well, I do,'' she snapped. ''I don't intend to lose my house, Mr. Delaney, no matter who it belongs to. Now, just what are your intentions?''

''I haven't got any. Not yet, anyway.''

''But…''

''Look.'' Delaney eased his boots off the desktop and sat upright. ''I moved in because it didn't make sense to keep paying rent at the hotel. Other than that, I haven't made any decisions.''

''Do you expect half the income from my boarders?'' she asked.

''I expect to have a bed to sleep on. Period. That's

it. I don't need clean sheets. Hell, lady, I don't even need sheets.''

"Don't be absurd," Hannah replied with a sniff. "Since you're living there, you'll be treated like any other of my boarders. Clean linens every week. Coffee and toast if you want them in the morning. Dinner at six o'clock. Noon on Sundays.''

He laughed and shook his head, further infuriating Hannah. Everything she'd planned to say had come out different. She'd wanted to resolve her problem, but now instead of being resolved, it seemed more complicated. And irritating.

"Did I say something funny?" she asked.

"Not exactly, but you sound a lot like a sergeant I had when I was in the army, Mrs. Dancer." He grinned. "What time's reveille?"

Hannah stood up and began stabbing her fingers into her gloves. "I don't find it all that amusing. It's not just a house, Mr. Delaney, no matter who it belongs to. It's a business. And as long as I'm in charge of it, I intend to keep it running smoothly.''

She turned and walked to the door. "Dinner's at six," she said, twisting the knob. "We'll be expecting you.''

Then she slammed the door behind her.

At five-forty-five, Delaney was washing up in the jailhouse's tin washbasin, muttering curses as he went along, and then having to spit out the bubbles of harsh lye soap that found their way into his mouth with every other oath he swore.

He glared into the dirty, cracked mirror above the washbasin. "'It's not a house but a business!' Well, it sure as hell isn't *my* business, Hannah Dancer.''

She never had gotten around to stating her proposition. At least Delaney didn't think so. He'd been almost deafened by her looks, if such a thing was possible, and while she'd sat across from him listing numbers and schedules and the like, all he'd been able to think about was the stray wisp of red hair that curled against her cheek and the perfect column of her neck, so pale against her black collar.

Then, before he'd known what had hit him, she was up out of the chair and stomping out the jailhouse door, shouting that dinner would be at six and he'd damn well better be there.

It could have been worse, he supposed. Much worse. She could've refused to cooperate at all. She could've moved every stick of furniture out of his room this afternoon and let him come home to *his* house to sleep on *his* floor.

Actually, he was a little surprised the widow hadn't done exactly that. After all, her husband had left the contents of the house to her. Just as Delaney had a right to move in, Hannah had every right to strip his room right down to the floorboards and wallpaper.

She hadn't, though, had she?

Delaney dried his face. The mirror—broken before he'd ever come to Newton, and put together badly—

reflected his image in disparate halves, with his left eye a good inch higher than the right, his nose askew, and his mouth failing to meet in the center.

He laughed out loud. Come to think of it, it wasn't so different from the way Hannah Dancer made him feel.

Hannah surveyed the serving plates on the table in the kitchen. The roast pork was perfectly done. The summer squash was tender and steaming. The biscuits were fine on top, but Nancy had burned the bottoms.

Hannah couldn't remember when she'd fussed so over a simple dinner. But this evening she had. She told herself it wasn't because she wanted to please Delaney, but rather that she didn't want to accidentally poison the man and be accused of murder.

But, in truth, she did want to please him. The more he liked living here, the less inclined he'd feel to sell the place. Or so she hoped.

"I'll take the biscuits and butter into the dining room, Nancy. Will you bring in the rest?"

"Too many biscuits," the girl said. "That's why I burned 'em. Why'd you have me make so many?"

"Because we have an extra guest for dinner. I thought I told you. Sheriff Delaney has moved in and will be taking his meals here from now on."

"I guess that means more wash." Nancy gave a little snort and rolled her eyes.

"No, Nancy. As a matter of fact, it doesn't. The wash will be the same as when Mr. Dancer was alive.'' Hannah narrowed her eyes on the young woman. ''So don't be hounding me for more money, do you hear? We upped your wages just a few months ago. Even that's more than you deserve for all the complaining you do.''

The girl snorted again while Hannah snatched up the biscuits and butter, then headed for the dining room, wishing she had a free hand to smooth back her hair. Oh, well. What difference did it make? She wanted Delaney to enjoy the food, not her.

Instead of being seated in their customary chairs, everyone was milling around the table. Delaney included. Hannah hadn't realized she was so anxious about his arrival until she actually saw him.

''Sit,'' Hannah said. ''Dinner's ready.''

No one moved. Well, no one except Abel Fairfax, who stood rocking back and forth on the balls of his feet.

''Sit. Please.''

''We don't know where,'' Miss Green piped up.

''For heaven's sake, Florence. You've been sitting in the same chair for nearly two years.'' Hannah put the biscuits and butter dish down with a thump. ''Whatever is the matter?''

''Well…'' the teacher stammered.

''He is.'' Henry Allen jerked his thumb toward Delaney. ''I said it isn't right for him to sit in Mr. Dancer's place.''

Oh, dear. Hannah hadn't given that a thought, nor had she anticipated Henry's sudden and rather vehement territorial instincts. This wasn't good at all. But before she could think of a solution, the sheriff spoke.

"I'm partial to a seat where I can keep an eye on the door." He pulled out the chair beside Abel's. "This'll do fine."

Hannah gave silent thanks to the heavens, then said, "Well, then. Now that that's settled, it's time for dinner."

Henry made a great show of pulling out her chair and seating her, a gesture he seemed to be performing more and more of late. And this time, Hannah could have sworn she felt his fingertips brush her shoulders before he took his own customary seat next to Miss Green.

Dinner had been a disaster, to Hannah's way of thinking.

Nancy had been unusually surly, slapping the serving dishes down as if they were playing cards, then slamming back into the kitchen and rattling pots and pans.

Florence Green had twittered like a canary during the entire meal while Henry Allen had sulked and Abel Fairfax had worn an altogether inscrutable and irritating little grin. As for the sheriff, he didn't appear to notice the others' behavior. For the most part, he kept his eyes on his plate—when they weren't on the front door—and seemed to find his meal quite tasty.

Hannah's dinner had gone down in hunks, which was why she had left her bed at ten o'clock, downed a thimbleful of peppermint schnapps to settle her stomach, and then wandered out to the side porch for a bit of fresh air. It was a beautiful night, just cool enough to make Hannah pull her silk wrapper a bit closer around herself. A full moon cast a silver swathe across the lawn and glittered in the highest branches of the elms.

How she missed Ezra's quiet companionship. A night such as this would have found him out here, gazing up at the sky, thoughtfully smoking his pipe, taking advantage of the moonlight to read Tennyson or Sir Walter Scott.

"I couldn't sleep either."

Henry Allen's voice, so close behind her, startled her. Hannah whirled around and found herself standing nearly toe to toe with the young banker. She took a step backward.

"You frightened me, Henry. I didn't hear you coming."

"Sorry. I didn't mean to. It's just that…" He fell silent for a moment, gazing at her like a lovesick boy. "It's just that I saw you standing out here in the moonlight and…"

Oh, don't, Hannah thought. *Please don't.* She'd tried so hard not to encourage him. She'd tried, in fact, to discourage him. Despite all her efforts, though, here he was, blushing, stammering, about to reveal his innermost feelings and expose a heart that she could only hurt.

"My dear." He took a step toward her, his eyes

shining with hope and desire. "My dearest Mrs. Dancer." His arms rose in an attempt to embrace her.

Hannah retreated again, but this time she backed up against the porch rail. There was nowhere left to go.

"Henry," she began rather sternly only to be cut off by her lovestruck suitor.

"No. Please let me speak, let me—"

A different voice, far deeper than Henry's, sounded from nearby.

"Evening."

Delaney emerged from the shadows. Moonlight glanced off the barrel of the shotgun cradled in his arms.

It took barely a second for Henry's expression to change from ardor to astonishment and then to outright embarrassment. Despite the darkness, Hannah could tell his face was fairly flaming. He'd just been caught in an obvious effort to seduce her, and caught by the sheriff, of all people.

Thank heaven! Hannah nearly wanted to laugh.

"Well, it's getting...it's late," Henry stammered. "I believe I'll retire." He spun on his heel and, without so much as a glance backward, almost sprinted through the front door.

While Henry was making his exit, Delaney came up the steps of the side porch. Hannah was getting used to the soft music of his spurs. The sound was oddly comforting.

She perched on the railing, once again drawing her wrapper more closely about her.

"You're up late, Delaney." She cocked her head and smiled. "Making sure all the fine folks of Newton are safe and sound asleep in their beds?"

"Most of them anyway."

His comment could have been construed as amusing had there been the slightest glint of amusement in his eyes or about his mouth, but there was no mirth at all in his iron-dark eyes or the rigid set of his lips. His disapproval of the scene he had just witnessed was apparent.

"Thank you for rescuing me from that uncomfortable situation," she said. "Henry's very young, and…"

"Impressionable?" The word came out more like an accusation than a question.

"Well, yes, I suppose…"

"I'd watch what I wore at midnight under a full moon, then, if I were you." As if to underscore his meaning, Delaney's eyes travelled the length of Hannah's pale silk wrapper—a slow and keen appraisal—before returning to her face.

Hannah's shoulders stiffened and her chin came up. "I'll wear what I choose, Sheriff, and when I choose. How others react to that isn't my concern."

He shifted the shotgun slightly. The grim set of his mouth eased into a small smile. "That's a fine notion, ma'am, and if you lived in an ivory tower, I guess it would suffice. But you wander around like that here…'' He angled his head, indicating her wrapper, ''…and you best be prepared to deal with the consequences.''

''The consequences!'' Hannah was furious, rising from her perch on the railing as if it had caught on fire. Why, the man was clearly accusing her of out-and-out seduction, as if she'd deliberately dressed this way to lure poor Henry Allen.

''The consequences!'' she screeched. ''I take it you're referring to young Mr. Allen.''

Delaney didn't answer immediately, but when he did his voice wasn't much more than a rough whisper.

''Him, too.''

''Too?'' It was all Hannah could say before her mouth fell open as if her jaw had come loose at the hinges. Then, as much as she wanted to flee, she couldn't break her gaze away from the man who'd just confessed his own attraction to her.

He stood there, silent, his frank, bold stare reiterating what he'd just told her. *I want you,* his eyes said.

Hannah's hand fluttered to her throat. She couldn't help but wonder what her own eyes were saying in return or whether or not Delaney could tell her heart was beating so fast it was threatening to pop right out of her chest. She could hardly breathe.

Delaney gave a soft laugh. ''Well, I wouldn't lose any sleep over it, if I were you.'' He tugged politely at the brim of his hat as he walked past her toward the front door. ''Good night, Mrs. Dancer.''

Chapter Nine

"Liar."

Delaney muttered the word like a curse at the same time he drove a fist into his pillow, rearranging it yet again in an effort to fall asleep.

It wasn't his habit to lie—to women or to men— just to save himself from embarrassment or from a confrontation. In fact, he'd always prided himself on his willingness to face the consequences of his words or his actions, whatever those might have been.

He never intended to make his feelings known to the widow. Not even if he could have figured out just what those feelings were. But, tonight, there she'd been, dressed in silk, swathed in moonlight. And there he'd been, standing in the shadows, watching her, wanting her, watching while the smitten young banker made his clumsy move, and feeling jealousy burn through his body like a fever.

Delaney tried to console himself with the fact that he hadn't lied completely. He'd given Hannah a pretty good indication of his desire, and he could tell from her eyes that she hadn't misread his look. That was truth in its boldest form. But the lie had been in letting her think that those feelings meant nothing to him, that they weren't worth losing sleep over.

Maybe it was the portrait that was keeping him awake. He opened one eye and positioned his head to watch moonlight and the shadows of elm leaves moving on the surface of Hannah's painted dress. The blue velvet seemed almost real, the woman inside it preparing to step out of her gilded frame.

If she did, he wondered, would she be surprised to find him in her husband's bed? Or would she be pleased, would she come to him and…?

He heard a rustling then coming from the dressing room that connected Hannah's room with Ezra's. His room now. Delaney's heart held absolutely still. If, by some miracle, she came to him, would he have the courage or the will to turn her away?

After a few moments of eternity, he heard the soft thunk of a metal bolt, but he hadn't a clue whether it was being opened for him or barred against him.

He lay there a long time, breathing deeply, wondering, not really wanting to know.

As soon as he awoke the next morning, Delaney could tell from the slant of the sun that he'd overslept by at least three hours. His pocket watch confirmed it when he snatched it off the nightstand and glared at its face. Ten minutes after nine. Dammit to hell, he swore. If he'd slept so damn late, why did he still feel so exhausted?

The widow Dancer smirked at him from the safety of her frame on the wall. That ancient, almost mythological smile of hers seemed to mock him this morning, so Delaney dressed with his back to the portrait, fumbling with his buttons as he did every day. After deciding not to shave—might just as well look as wrung-out as he felt—he picked up his shotgun and went downstairs.

A high-pitched female voice called from the dining room. "Oh, Sheriff Delaney. Is that you?"

He was sorely tempted to ignore the schoolmarm and walk straight out the door, but he turned left toward the dining room where Miss Green was sitting in her customary place. Across the table from her was a shaggy-haired stranger, however. Delaney didn't like the looks of him one bit or the bullet-laden bandolier that slanted across the man's chest.

"Oh, here he is, Mr. Weller," Miss Green twittered. "Sheriff Delaney, may I introduce Mr. Cleveland Weller, come all the way from Tombstone, Arizona."

The man stood up and extended his hand. "Name's Cleve Weller. How do."

Delaney shook his hand, noting that in addition to the bandolier, the man also wore a Colt Peacemaker on his right hip and a knife on his left. "You're packing a lot of artillery for a quiet Kansas town, aren't you, Weller?"

The man laughed. "Truth is, I feel naked without it." He glanced at Florence Green, who was blushing furiously now. "No offense, ma'am."

"Well, I don't mean to offend you, Weller," Delaney said, "but I'm going to have to ask you to stow the pistol away or leave it at the jailhouse. Town ordinance. No carrying of firearms."

"Just like Dodge," Weller grumbled.

"Just like Dodge." Delaney hoped that would put an end to any argument the man might try. Everybody knew that in Dodge City to carry a firearm was risking the wrath not to mention the hard muscle of the law. His job in Newton had been a lot easier as a result of his reputation in Dodge.

Of course, Weller didn't know that Delaney's right hand and arm weren't worth much these days. If the man chose to ignore the warning or test the limits of the law…

"I didn't come here looking for trouble." Weller put on an affable smile as he began unbuckling his gun belt. "Fact is, Sheriff, I came here looking for you." He folded the ends of the belt around his holster and handed the neat leather package to Delaney. Still smiling, he added, "I guess I can tolerate feeling naked for one day."

Just as he was saying that, Hannah came through the door from the kitchen, a pot of coffee in her hand.

"More coffee, Mr. Weller? I see you've already met the sheriff."

"Yes, ma'am, I have. And I'll take some more of

that coffee, too.'' Cleve Weller pulled out his chair, preparing to sit.

Before his seat had quite made contact, however, Delaney said, ''We'll have coffee at the office after I stow this weapon. Come on.''

''Well, now…'' Weller seemed to almost hover above the chair.

It didn't take a mind reader to see that the stranger far preferred to take his morning coffee with two women, one of them a beautiful redhead, rather than with an unshaven, ill-tempered lawman. And it didn't take Delaney more than a few seconds to decide that leaving Cleveland Weller here to sip coffee while making eyes at Hannah was the last thing he was going to do.

''Coffee, Sheriff?'' she asked.

''No, thanks. Let's go, Weller.''

Delaney headed toward the front door, relieved to hear a flurry of goodbyes behind him—Miss Green's being the loudest and the longest—and then the tromp of the stranger's boots following him out the door.

Hannah filled a cup from the pot in her hand and then sat in the chair that had just been vacated by the stranger.

''Where did he say he came from?'' she asked Miss Green, who was still staring rather dreamily in the direction of the front door.

''Tombstone. In Arizona Territory. Can you imagine a town named Tombstone?''

Unfortunately, Hannah could. Newton had been a wild young town briefly, full of longhorn cattle and cowboys determined to make up for months without women or drink. Plenty of those young men remained here in the little graveyard called the Weed Patch. For a while in those early years, long before Florence's arrival, Newton could've been called Tombstone, too.

"He's quite dashing, don't you think?" the school-teacher asked.

Hannah stared at Miss Green. The young woman's plump and characteristically pale face was red as a radish now.

"Why, Florence!" Hannah laughed, then leaned across the table to whisper, "I do believe you're smitten with Mr. Cleveland Weller."

Miss Green's blush deepened, which Hannah didn't believe possible, and her eyes fairly glittered. "Oh, no. I didn't mean that rough Mr. Weller," she said. "I was referring to the sheriff. I've never in all my life seen a man quite so...so..."

"Dashing," Hannah finished for her a bit more sourly than she'd intended, mindful of a little stitch that pulled tight in her stomach at the mere mention of Delaney.

"I'm such a goose." Miss Green twisted her napkin on her lap and gazed soulfully at Hannah. "I shouldn't have said anything, but... You won't tell anyone, will you, Mrs. Dancer? Oh, please. I should simply die if—"

"No, Florence. I won't tell a soul. Your secret is absolutely safe with me."

Miss Green pushed her chair back and stood. "I really must go," she said. "I have an appointment this morning, and I fear I'm already late. Esther Chapman is fitting me for a new dress."

"Well, go along then. Tell Esther I said..."

But the schoolteacher had already bustled out of the dining room before Hannah could quite get out the word "hello." She dawdled over her coffee then, staring out the window at nothing in particular, wondering why she suddenly felt so peevish and unsettled.

Florence Green was in love with Delaney! That had escaped Hannah's attention completely. She wondered now if the sheriff had exhibited a similar passion for the schoolmarm that she had also failed to see. Had he? And all the while she had thought...no, she had wished...longed...

Close behind her, Nancy cleared her throat in an obvious attempt to get Hannah's attention.

"I said I'll do up the last of the breakfast dishes whenever you're done in here," the hired girl said.

Hannah's thoughts snapped back to the here and now. She felt her face burning nearly as crimson as the teacher's had only moments before.

"Thank you, Nancy. I'm done."

Done being foolish, Hannah said to herself, then snatched up her cup and saucer and followed Nancy into the kitchen.

* * *

Cleve Weller was sitting across the desk from Delaney, both men leaning back in their chairs, boots atop the stained, paper-strewn blotter.

Delaney was thinking that maybe his first impression of the man had been off the mark. As it turned out, Weller had arrived in Tombstone around the same time as the Earps and thrown in his lot with the brothers and Doc Holliday. He had come to Kansas to collect a debt, and had agreed to do Wyatt a favor in passing a message along to Delaney.

"I had a hell of a time finding you," Weller was saying now. "If I didn't know you were such a good friend of Wyatt's, I'd've quit inquiring in Dodge after the seventh person told me they didn't know your whereabouts. Lucky for you I fell into conversation with a pretty little blond faro dealer by the name of Crystal who pointed me in this direction." Weller winked. "Crystal sends her sweet affections and kind regards, by the way."

Delaney merely nodded. He tried conjuring up a mental image of Crystal, but he couldn't. There had been more than a few blondes over the years.

"You said you had a message from Wyatt?"

"He said to tell you he's sorely in need of good men in Tombstone. There are some boys out there who aren't partial to anyone's laws but their own. And there's a county sheriff who doesn't care a whole lot for the Earps and doesn't care who knows it."

It was an appeal that a year earlier Delaney would have responded to in an instant, but now…

"Wyatt also said you were one of the best men with a gun he'd ever had the pleasure of working with." Weller frowned, then glanced at the shotgun leaning against the desk. "I see you're carrying a side-by-side now."

"It's a pretty quiet town." That was true enough, Delaney thought, though it wasn't the whole truth.

It was also true that he was one of the best men with a gun that Wyatt had ever worked with. Was. But that didn't mean he couldn't be again, with a little more time and a lot more practice. The invitation to Tombstone was more than a little appealing at the moment.

It was heaven-sent. His feelings for Hannah—the ones he'd been somewhat successful in ignoring— were beginning to get out of hand, he decided, remembering the jealous stab in his gut when he'd seen her with the amorous young banker last night, and then again, just this morning, when this Weller fellow had appeared at her table. It wasn't good, he warned himself again, getting so confounded proprietary about a woman.

Wyatt needed him. That was reason enough to break his contract with the town of Newton. He was tempted to tell Cleve Weller then and there that he'd be in Tombstone just as fast as he could. Still, he didn't want to appear too eager. And there was the everpresent matter of cold, hard cash to be taken care of.

"How soon are you going back to Arizona?" Delaney asked.

Weller seemed thoughtful for a moment as he scratched his shaggy head. "Well, I was thinking about starting out tomorrow. But I'll tell you, after seeing that pretty redhead this morning..."

"She's spoken for."

"Is that so?" The man eyed Delaney curiously for a second, then shrugged. "In that case, then I probably will head back southwest tomorrow."

Good riddance, Delaney thought, while he once again castigated himself for being so infernally territorial where the widow was concerned. It was definitely time to get out of town, he thought, and he was about to communicate that to Weller when a bullet shattered the glass on the front window of the jailhouse.

He didn't know who moved faster. But both men's boots came up off the desktop and they rolled out of their chairs and onto the floor before all the window glass had tinkled from its frame.

"You all right?" Delaney asked.

"Yeah. Christ. I thought you said this was a quiet town."

There was considerable shouting out on the street now, and the men crept to the broken window to peer out. A curse ripped through the sheriff's teeth when he saw who was to blame for the errant bullet.

"You know him?" Weller asked.

"Seth Akins," Delaney growled. "He hits the bottle every now and again, beats the bejesus out of his wife, then puts up a good show of trying to kill himself.''

''Well, it looks like more than a show this time.''

That it did. Akins was standing in the middle of the street with a gun pointed at his head while his wife and sons cowered in the back of a nearby wagon.

''Damned fool,'' Delaney muttered. He crept back to the desk and retrieved his shotgun. Out of habit, he broke it open to make sure it was loaded.

''You figure you're going to solve this with that blunderbuss?'' Weller asked, eying the shotgun rather contemptuously while reaching to the desk for the pistol Delaney had confiscated from him earlier. ''Here. Use this. You can pick that gun right out of his hand before he knows what's hit him. And if you miss…hell, you're probably doing the world a favor.''

It was true, and nobody knew that better than the sheriff. A single well-aimed pistol shot would end the confrontation one way or another. A year ago that's exactly what he would have done. But now…

''The hell with it.'' Weller raised his arm, squinted, and fired his gun out the broken window.

Seth Akins fell like a tree.

''He won't be bothering his missus or his boys or much of anybody anymore.'' The man from Tombstone turned away from the window and handed his gun over to Delaney. ''I'll let you take the credit, Sheriff. And I'll keep quiet when I get back to Arizona.'' Weller smirked. ''Hell, Wyatt would be real disappointed to hear you lost your nerve.''

Instead of taking the gun from him, though, Delaney—slowly, oh so slowly—leveled his shotgun on the man's belt buckle.

''You keep it, Weller. You'll need it.'' He angled his head toward the rear of the office. ''There's a door just past the last cell. Use it, and don't come back to my town.''

Weller's expression didn't change as he went through the slow and deliberate movements of putting his gun belt on and tying down his holster. Delaney knew he was calculating the odds of a Colt against a side-by-side at a distance of two feet.

He couldn't say he was all that surprised when the man concluded he'd be better off—not to mention still breathing—by choosing to leave by the back door.

By the time Delaney reached the fallen Seth Akins, a small crowd had already gathered. Mayor Staub, to nobody's surprise, immediately grabbed the opportunity to make a speech about law and order in Newton.

''The sheriff was right to do what he did,'' Staub was saying. ''Why, we can't have every Tom, Dick, and Harry waving pistols in the middle of town, threatening our women and children.''

He pointed to Mrs. Akins and her sons where they still sat, appearing stupefied, in the back of their battered wagon.

Delaney elbowed past the mayor and knelt beside
Akins's body. He tested the man's neck for a pulse.
"Somebody go get the undertaker," he said quietly,
not loud enough for Akins's wife and boys to hear.

"The town council will have an inquiry, Sheriff,
but I can tell you already that there won't be any
charges," the mayor said. "Quite frankly, the scoun-
drel was asking for it."

Delaney didn't answer. He stood and walked to the
Akins's wagon.

"Ma'am," he said, taking off his hat. "I meant
only to shoot the gun out of his hand. It wasn't my
intention to bring your husband down."

The woman's eyes were dry and her voice was flat
as she responded. "You did what you had to do, I
guess." She picked up the reins and gave them a
shake over the back of the mule. "It's over now. And
I'm sorry about that slap I gave you. See to his burial,
Sheriff, will you? I'm taking my boys home now."

"Yes, ma'am." Delaney stepped back before the
wagon wheel could roll over his toes. "If you need
anything, you or your boys, just let me know," he
called after her, but Mrs. Akins's only reply was a
shake of her head and a weary shrug.

Then someone tapped his arm and said quietly,
"That gunshot just about emptied every house and
business in town."

Delaney turned to see Abel Fairfax pointing his
chin in the direction of the Dancer house, where Hannah was standing on the edge of the lawn.

"I believe she's worried about you," Fairfax said. "What do you think?"

He thought he would have laughed out loud if it weren't for the circumstances. Delaney just sighed instead, then jammed his hat on his head before he answered, "I think she's probably wishing the poor devil lying there in the street was me."

Chapter Ten

Nancy spent the better part of the day jabbering about the shooting. In fact, she went on and on so incessantly that Hannah finally let the girl go home early and peeled the potatoes herself in blessed silence, trying her best to forget about the shooting, to forget how her heart had leapt into her throat at the sound of the gunshot, and how it had remained there until she saw that it wasn't Delaney face down in the dusty street. Only later had it occurred to her—with an accompanying rush of guilt—that his sudden and violent demise would solve her problem with the house.

And she was still feeling a twinge of guilt when she joined the sheriff and Abel Fairfax at the dinner table later that evening. Then, no sooner had she announced that Henry Allen was working late at the bank and Miss Green was having supper with her dressmaker, than Abel claimed to have gotten a sudden and fierce migraine that forced him to repair to his room.

In all the years that Abel had boarded there, Hannah had never known the man to be unwell or even stricken with anything more severe than occasional dyspepsia. She was, therefore, distinctly alarmed when the older man shot up from his place at the table, dropped his napkin, and headed toward the stairs.

"Is there anything I can do to help you, Abel?" she asked. She had already folded her own napkin and was about to accompany him, but Abel pressed his hand on her shoulder to prevent her from standing.

"No. No. You stay here, my dear. I'll be fine. It's nothing, really. I'll return once I've taken a headache powder."

He moved very fast then, Hannah thought, for a man with a blinding headache, and from the staircase he called back, "I'm sure the two of you can find plenty to talk about while I'm gone."

Could they?

Would they?

Hannah looked down the table where Delaney sat in the chair next to Abel's vacant one. Her heart promptly bounded into her throat, so much so that Hannah feared she wouldn't be able to swallow a single bite of her supper. Not that it mattered. Her appetite had suddenly vanished. And so had whatever gift she once had possessed for conversation, apparently.

Just what did one say to a man who had shot and
killed someone only a few hours earlier? How was
your day, Sheriff?

As it turned out, she didn't have to worry because
it was Delaney who spoke first.

"I get the feeling I unsettle you, Mrs. Dancer."
His fork was midway between his plate and his
mouth, hovering over his plate. "Maybe it's got
something to do with that Akins business today?" He
angled his head slightly, finished the bite of ham on
his fork, and chewed it thoughtfully.

Hannah was, in truth, more than a little unsettled,
but she feared it had nothing at all to do with the
shooting. Sitting a bit straighter in her chair, she replied as coolly as she could, "I've seen men shot
before, Sheriff. Here in Kansas. And back in Mississippi during the war. I haven't spent my entire
twenty-eight years in a glass case, you know."

"No, ma'am. I didn't think you had." His mouth
quirked in the smallest of grins. "Tell me about Mississippi."

Hannah blinked. "I beg your pardon?"

"Mississippi," he said, juggling his knife and fork
to cut another bite of ham. "Tell me about it. Do you
still have family there?"

"No, I…"

She'd spent so many years trying to forget those
ugly, painful, dirt-poor times, trying to pretend they'd
never happened at all. Ezra never mentioned them.
He knew better. Well, Ezra knew the truth.

"Sorry," Delaney said then, obviously aware of her discomfort. "I just thought, since we're stuck together in this house business, it might help if we got to know each other some. I wasn't prying, Mrs. Dancer. Just forget I asked."

"I didn't mean to be rude, Mr. Delaney. It's just that I rarely, if ever, think of my life before Ezra came along. My family wasn't well off before the war, and afterwards our circumstances went from bad to worse. If there is anyone left in Mississippi, I haven't been in contact with them after all these years."

He nodded and continued his meal in silence, keeping his eyes on his plate.

"Well, I didn't mean we shouldn't become better acquainted," Hannah said. "As you said, we are rather shackled together by this house for the time being."

She sat back in her chair now and pushed her untouched plate away. "Tell me about you, Delaney. About yourself. Where do you come from?"

"Illinois."

Hannah waited for him to continue, but he didn't.

She pressed on. "Then I assume you took part in the war."

After he nodded, she laughed softly. "So, we were enemies, then."

"No," he said, his autumn-colored gaze turning quite somber as it played over her face. "Never enemies. Not you and me."

When she felt a flush spreading upward from her

bosom to her face, Hannah looked away. She wanted this man to be her enemy because the alternative was too frightening, too terrifying to even consider.

"Hannah," he said quietly. "Don't worry."

She met his gaze, still piercing, but now glinting with a curious humor.

"It's not going to happen," he said.

"What?"

"Us."

She felt her face burning now, and though she wanted to look away she couldn't. Those deep hazel eyes held her fast.

"I don't..." she stammered. "I don't understand."

"Yes, you do." Delaney pushed his plate away, then rose from his chair and slid it back under the table with a kind of finality. "I'm going back to work."

"But you didn't finish..."

He was gone before the words were out of her mouth, though, and Hannah sat there for the longest time, trying not to think, willing herself not to feel. Not the heat of her flesh. Not the pounding of her heart. Not the emptiness of the room now that Delaney was gone. Not anything.

When Delaney got back to the jailhouse, his deputy, Lionel Cole, was slanted back in a chair out in front, studying the sunset as if it were the first time he'd ever seen one. He pulled up another chair beside the young man and fastened his own gaze on the banners of brilliant orange and fiery red in the western sky.

"Sure is pretty, ain't it, Sheriff?"

"Sure is, Lionel. Why don't you go home and share it with that pretty little wife of yours? I'll take over here."

"You mean it?"

"Yep. Go on."

The deputy didn't have to be told twice. After he left, Delaney stayed out on the sidewalk, contemplating the beauty of the end of day. There had been a time when he'd looked forward to sunsets because they signalled the beginning of wild and reckless nights, his own before he was a lawman, and then after, when the prospect of night was also the prospect of danger and excitement. Now his nights weren't so different from his days. Quieter, even. Lonelier. That was for certain.

He made a disgusted little clucking sound with his tongue and shifted in his chair. Since when, he wondered, had he given a moment's thought to loneliness? Since when did sending a deputy home to spend an evening with his wife make Delaney feel not just alone, but empty as well?

The answer was pretty obvious. Since Hannah Dancer had taken up residence in his thoughts and driven out everything else. No woman had ever occupied his every waking moment the way she did. Not even when he was a boy and so smitten with Caroline that he walked five extra miles in any weather just to see her home from school each day and to steal a gentle, blushing kiss. Hell, he'd never even kissed Hannah. Dammit.

All of a sudden, sitting there all alone, Delaney found himself grinning like a fool. That was the problem, of course. He hadn't kissed her. That was why the woman was such a torment, why she continually haunted his brain. And the solution was so easy that he wondered why he hadn't thought of it before.

He'd kiss her, and then the spell she'd somehow cast over him would be gone. One taste of her pretty mouth would prove that she was just like any other woman, and then her magical hold on him would be gone.

He'd just go ahead and kiss her. That's exactly what he'd do.

Maybe tomorrow.

No.

Tonight.

Hannah sighed and threw the bedcovers back. She'd tossed and turned for hours, it seemed. Long enough to hear Henry Allen return from his late night at the bank. Long enough to hear Florence Green's footsteps on the stairs an hour after that when she returned from her evening of socializing with her dressmaker friend.

If Delaney had come home, she hadn't heard him. But that was no surprise. The man could move as silently as smoke when he wanted to.

She felt like the only person on earth who was still awake. It was time, she decided, to go downstairs and pour herself a thimbleful, two perhaps, of Ezra's soothing peppermint schnapps.

Not bothering with her wrapper, she slipped down the dark hallway and descended the stairs, careful to avoid the one that creaked. She eased open the pocket door to the front parlor just enough to pass through. It was quiet, except for the ticking of the mantel clock. Moonlight sifted through the sheer lace curtains and lit a wide swath across the Persian carpet. Hannah followed that silver path to the table against the far wall where she filled a small glass with what she hoped would be a swift and potent sleeping draught.

The clear liquor burned down the back of her throat. Blinking back a sheen of tears, she poured herself a second shot and lifted the little glass to her lips.

"Better not make a habit out of that."

Hannah whirled in the direction of the deep voice, sweet liquor spilling down the front of her gown while her heart leapt into her throat. Delaney stood in the narrow doorway, moonlight glossing his black boots, glinting in his eyes, silvering the slight smile on his lips.

"You startled me." Hannah clutched the now empty glass to her chest, vaguely aware that the bodice of her thin cotton gown was wet and sticky with schnapps.

He didn't apologize. He didn't say a word, but only stood there looking at her.

Hannah didn't speak either. She couldn't. It was all she could do to breathe while her heart pounded and seemed to take up every inch of space in her chest and while her head suddenly felt woozy and light.

"You all right?" Delaney finally asked, breaking the silence but not breaking his intense gaze.

"Yes." Hannah put the glass down on the table. No, she wasn't all right. Her legs felt weak now and she wasn't at all certain that she'd be able to walk out of the parlor or climb the stairs without using both hands on the bannister. She had to try, though. The alternative was standing there in a wet, sticky night-dress until she fainted dead away under that relentless scrutiny.

"Well, then. Good night." Her voice felt as weak as her knees as she began to cross what now appeared to be a mile or two of intricate carpet.

She reminded Delaney of the woman in the portrait as she came through the moonlight. Only she had stepped out of her blue velvet dress when she had stepped out of the frame, and she was wearing a gown of translucent white that allowed her feminine shape to shine through.

He stood there spellbound, his heart battering his rib cage, his breath caught in his throat. Then, as she neared, Delaney remembered his intention to kiss her. Tonight.

Instinctively, he raised his hand to grasp the edge

of the pocket door in order to bar her exit, but then he immediately cursed himself because he was sure that his injured hand and its feeble grip wouldn't be able to deter a willful child from skipping out of the parlor, much less a full-grown woman with leaving foremost on her mind.

It was going to take Hannah about one second, one small but determined flick of her wrist, to remove the obstacle in her path, and Delaney knew that that shameful defeat would wither his intention of tasting her beautiful mouth tonight so that he might be able to forget it tomorrow.

But she didn't flick her wrist or even attempt to brush his arm aside. Instead, after she had crossed the parlor's moonlit path, she stopped—her bare toes just inches from his boots, her face just inches from the buttons on his waistcoat. She was so close that he could see the hectic beat of her heart where it pulsed just above the neckline of her gown. She stood so close now that every breath he drew in was heavy with her scent. Roses and musk and just a hint of peppermint.

With his good hand, he tipped her chin up. She didn't resist. Nor did she flinch or look away when he curved his arm around and brought her even closer against him. It was then he could feel the feathery trembling all through her, but whether it was desire or fear, Delaney couldn't have guessed.

"It's all right, Hannah," he whispered, dipping his head, just touching his lips to hers.

For a stunned moment, the softness of her mouth amazed him. He couldn't remember ever having kissed a woman with such gentleness as he was kissing Hannah now. As if her lips were butterfly wings, about to break beneath his touch. His own restraint amazed him. Then his tongue grazed across her mouth and he savored the minty, sticky residue of the liquor she had quaffed. The taste very nearly made him drunk. The touch made him dizzy. Delaney deepened the kiss.

Hannah meant to say "no," but she moaned softly instead. What had the sheriff just said? "It's all right, Hannah?" It wasn't all right—not at all—but even so she couldn't refrain from drawing closer to his warmth and couldn't stop herself from responding to his kiss.

It had been so long since…

No, that wasn't true. Not so long, but never at all. Never had a kiss affected her so. Never had a kiss touched not just her lips but her very soul.

Both of his arms encircled her now and the heat of his body burned through her thin gown and threatened to melt everything inside her. She had known it would be like this. From the very first moment she laid eyes on this man, she had somehow known just how easily he would be able to set her on fire. To burn her.

Hannah turned her head to escape his ravishing mouth. "No," she said, shocked at the huskiness of her own voice. "We mustn't. Let me go."

But he didn't. Delaney held her tighter instead, and tighter still with every hard breath he took.

"Hannah," he whispered roughly, following her name with a muted curse.

"Let me go. Please. This is wrong."

"Wrong?" Delaney shook his head. "Nothing's ever felt so right."

It was true, Hannah thought. And for a split second she was about to agree, about to willingly and joyously melt in his embrace. But then Delaney let her go.

He took a slow step back into the vestibule, out of her way. The expression on his face was as somber as Hannah had ever seen and he drew in a long breath before he said, "I won't apologize, Hannah. If you want to slap my face, go ahead. I won't stop you."

She might have if she thought for a second that it would erase what had just happened or make her forget how this man's kiss had made her feel. Wicked and wanting and wonderful. When she lifted her hand, not to slap him but to gently touch his cheek, Delaney winced as if she had indeed delivered a blow. Then, without a word, he turned and walked up the stairs, never once looking back.

After jamming the pillows against the footboard, Delaney lay staring at the carved flowers of the walnut headboard. Moonlight edged each polished petal. He was counting them, again and again, like a man counting proverbial sheep in order to fall asleep. His endeavor wasn't meant to court sleep, however. It was purely a distraction from the portrait that loomed on the wall behind him.

He shouldn't have kissed her. Judas priest! What a dunderheaded, lamebrained, senseless thing to do. How in hell had he been so stupid as to believe that having Hannah—if only for a second—would make him want her less? That kiss, that moment he held her in his arms, had only made him want her more. For one long and aching eternity then, he had never wanted to let her go.

He held his right hand up, flexing it, opening it and closing it as if trying to catch moonlight. Which was about all that hand was good for these days, he thought morosely. There were worse ways, he supposed, to fail to be a whole man. After all, that bullet could just as easily have blasted off his foot or his kneecap or...well...he grimaced, considering the worst alternative.

Still, for a man who made his living with a gun, Delaney felt distinctly handicapped. And that was something he'd never ask a woman to share. Not a whole woman like Hannah, anyway.

He could feel her looking down on him from her frame. Hell, he could feel her breathing in the adjacent room. He could still taste her, all peppermint liquor and candied, succulent warmth. He'd taste her forever, no matter where he went or who else he kissed. Hannah Dancer's kiss would follow him to his grave.

To Tombstone.

For that was where he was going. First thing in the morning.

Alone.

Chapter Eleven

The next morning, although Hannah had hardly slept, she was up and bathed and perfectly dressed by six o'clock, even before Nancy arrived to get the oven going and put the big enamel coffeepot on a back burner of the stove.

Hannah had more energy this morning than she'd had in weeks. Too much perhaps. Every single nerve in her body felt like an overwound watch spring while her lips kept creeping upward in a smile which she continually, and unsuccessfully, attempted to suppress.

Like it or not, she had to admit that the source of all her energy was Delaney's kiss the night before. And contrary to her better judgment, she couldn't wait to see him this morning.

"Foolish," she muttered just as Nancy came in the back door with a basket of eggs in one hand and a bouquet of cornflowers and Queen Anne's lace in the other.

"T'ain't foolish," the girl said, giving the long stems a little shake. "Maybe they're nothing more than weeds to you, but I think they're awful pretty."

"I didn't mean the flowers, Nancy," Hannah said quickly. "I was just thinking out loud. Here." She snatched up a quart jar and pumped it full of water. "Let's put your lovely posies in here before they wilt."

Somewhat mollified, the girl stabbed the bouquet into the jar, then proceeded to put on her apron and grumpily tend to the stove while Hannah ground the coffee beans, all the while trying to tamp down on another of those dratted smiles.

Nancy picking flowers! Nancy who never even noticed such things. Now that was a first. What was the world coming to?

Then that same question reoccurred to her when she walked into the dining room and saw Florence Green, who this morning looked like anything but a schoolteacher. Her hair—a dishwater shade—was done up in a mass of curls, some of which dripped down her neck and at the side of her face. And that face! Florence was made up like…like a…well… courtesan was the kindest description that came to Hannah's mind.

"Florence!"

The teacher didn't reply, but rather stared at Hannah with a hint of belligerence in her eyes while she held her head stiffly so as not to dislodge her curls.

"You look…well…different." Now Hannah noticed that the bodice of the young woman's dress had been recut and resewn, the more to emphasize her bosom. And if Hannah wasn't mistaken, Florence's corset was pulled tighter—much tighter!—than was her habit.

Florence smiled. "I feel different," she said. "Better. By far." She sighed softly and then added brightly, almost coquettishly, "Has the sheriff come down for breakfast yet?"

"The sher—?" So that was it! The drab little spider was spinning a web to catch Delaney in! Hannah would have laughed if she hadn't thought it would hurt Florence's feelings, if she hadn't felt an odd stab of jealousy in the pit of her own stomach.

"No, he hasn't come down. Not yet. Would you like coffee this morning or tea?"

"Coffee, if you please."

Hannah went back to the kitchen where Nancy was sitting at the table, her nose buried in cornflowers and wild carrot blooms. The coffeepot wasn't even on its back burner yet.

"Nancy," she snapped. "I'm not paying you to sit and smell flowers, for heaven's sake."

When the girl jumped up and got busy, Hannah took her place at the table. Everyone in the house was behaving foolishly this morning, herself included. And whose fault was that? Who was it turning her house into a circus, an insane asylum, where people...female people...picked flowers and put on makeup and wore tight corsets and bemused expressions?

She cracked an egg into a bowl, then another and another. Her odd and irrepressible grin flattened out into a scowl now, and she found herself vaguely wishing she had slapped the audacious lawman the night before, yet at the same time keeping an eye on the door and an ear cocked in the direction of the staircase, listening for his footsteps and the soft metallic music of his spurs.

When Hannah went back into the dining room to pour the freshly brewed coffee, Henry Allen was sitting there, deep in conversation with Miss Green. Always the gentleman, he stood up and held Hannah's chair for her, but once she was seated the young banker didn't dither a moment or dally before returning to his own seat beside the newfangled, redesigned schoolteacher.

For a few minutes it was as if Hannah didn't exist, which should have pleased her no end, but bewildered her instead. It was a bit like being caught in a dream where familiar people did unfamiliar and quite uncharacteristic things.

And then she heard the faint jingle of spurs coming down the staircase at her back. Her heart fluttered like a butterfly, and she looked over her shoulder just in time to see Delaney place his carpetbag in the vestibule before coming into the dining room.

His carpetbag? The butterfly in Hannah's chest

stalled and seemed to turn to stone, thudding into her stomach.

"Mornin'," he said in that deep voice that seemed so familiar now, pulling out his chair and easing into it with what struck Hannah this morning as a particularly manly grace.

"Good morning, Sheriff," Miss Green trilled.

"Mornin', ma'am." His autumn-colored gaze rested on the schoolmarm a long moment. Warm. Appreciative. Not in the least perplexed by her provocative appearance.

Well, he was probably used to women making fools of themselves over him, Hannah thought.

"Nancy," she called, a bit too snappishly. "Please bring another cup of coffee."

The four of them sat in uncomfortable silence until Nancy banged through the door from the kitchen and plopped a cup and saucer in front of Delaney.

"Bread's about toasted," she said. "I'll bring it in a minute."

"None for me, thanks," Delaney said. He took a sip of the steaming brew, set his cup down, and stood up. "Can I have a word with you, Mrs. Dancer?" He angled his jaw toward the vestibule. "In private?"

"Yes. Of course." She tucked her napkin under her plate, allowed him to pull out her chair, then followed him into the hallway where that damned carpetbag now loomed large as a piece of furniture. Whatever did it mean?

She got her answer immediately.

"I'm leaving, Hannah."

"You're...?" Her eyes jerked up to his. "I don't understand."

"This house. Ezra's will. You." He shook his head. "It's all pure craziness."

"Yes, I know, but—"

"It's yours." He gestured around the vestibule, up the stairs. "All of it."

Hannah blinked. That was precisely what she wanted. Wasn't it? *Wasn't it?* But just then she felt so confused she didn't know what she wanted anymore. She didn't even know what to say, so that when she did speak the words came out as a total surprise.

"But you kissed me!"

Delaney looked a little off balance then, but only for a moment. "Yeah. I did." His left hand rose to cup her chin, lifting her face to his as if he just might do it again. His eyes closed briefly, and the expression on his face was a blend of wistfulness and sweet, painful longing.

Hannah held her breath.

But when he opened his eyes again, all that softness had disappeared. His face was stern once more. Hard as cast iron. Dark. Almost cruel. Even his whisper was harsh when he said, "It was a kiss goodbye."

He let go of her, reached for his shotgun and carpetbag, then walked out the door.

Delaney had barely walked half a block, muttering to himself all the while, when it occurred to him that

no matter how much he wanted to leave Newton—
leave today—this very second—it wasn't possible.
Not that he minded so much breaking the contract
he'd signed with the town, but what he couldn't bring
himself to do was leave several hundred decent town-
folk in the inexperienced, perhaps even incompetent
hands of his deputy, Lionel Cole.

He'd have to wait until a new lawman came to
town. Dammit. He could see how it was going to play
out already. The mayor and the town council would
dither and dawdle, hoping Delaney would change his
mind, and finally forcing him to go to Dodge City
and hire somebody away from the citizens there.

He should probably just head for Dodge today, thus
avoiding all the sorry business in between.

Sorry business, indeed. What was sorry was the
spectacle of a man walking away from a fortune because he was running away from a woman. That was
the truth, no matter how he tried to slice it. And he
wasn't going to change his mind, or stay any longer
than he had to.

He could feel the house behind him, perhaps even
Hannah gazing at his back. He'd seen the hurt in her
eyes when he told her that their only kiss had been
goodbye. She'd be better off without him. It wouldn't
take her long to realize that. Plus, she'd have her
house, which, Delaney was sure, was what she wanted
most.

He pushed through the door of his former residence, the National Hotal, and dropped his carpetbag in front of big Alma Spence's monumental desk.

"Any problem getting my old room back?" he asked.

"I rented it no more'n half an hour ago," she said without even glancing up from her paperwork. "Too bad for you."

"All right, then." He shifted his stance, settling his rifle on his shoulder, nudging up the brim of his hat. "I guess any other room would do."

"We're full up."

Delaney boiled silently, knowing full well that the woman was lying, that her primary source of entertainment was sticking pins in people's hides—particularly his. In light of his current mood, however, he decided this probably wasn't the best time to take on Big Alma Spence. Never in his life had he laid a hand on a woman other than with gentle love or energetic lust as the case might be, but there was always a first time, he feared, and considering Almighty Alma probably outweighed him by five or ten pounds, it might be an even match.

"Fine," he said, picking up his carpetbag, swearing under his breath. "I'll come back."

Alma snorted. Then she called to him just as he was going out the door. "Oh, I almost forgot. You just might be interested in the gentleman who's up there in your old room, Sheriff."

Delaney looked back. "Yeah? Why?"

"Name's Dancer." She grinned evilly. "Says he's Ezra's son."

One advantage to being sheriff, Delaney thought, was that it allowed a man to poke his nose in other people's business if he were so inclined. Ordinarily he wasn't, but the arrival of this Dancer fellow piqued his curiosity more than a little. Especially once he'd gotten a good look at him.

From his chair outside the jailhouse, Delaney had watched the man exit the hotel and make straight for the swinging doors of the Wild Horse Saloon. He dressed like a sporting man with a low-crowned hat, a bright tie and brocade vest, and fancy ruffles peeking out of his sleeves. Likely as not, there was a tidy roll of bills in his breast pocket and a dainty two-shot derringer tucked away somewhere on his person.

It was time, he figured, to pay an official call on the newcomer and maybe satisfy his own personal curiosity at the same time. He picked up his shotgun and sauntered across the street.

It was dark inside the Wild Horse. The air was thick and stale with tobacco smoke. The fact that it was morning made little or no impression on the several men standing at the bar or on the ones squinting across a poker table, trying to read the other players' expressions.

Dancer, it appeared, had already found himself a game. Delaney stepped up to the bar, where Charlie

Marsh was pushing a mug of steaming coffee across the bar top toward him.

"There you go, Sheriff," the wiry little barkeep said, adding with a wink, "Unless you're in the mood for something stronger."

Delaney laughed. "Nothing's as strong as your coffee, Charlie." He took a sip. "You know anything about that fella over there?"

The little man shrugged. "Nope. He didn't say a word when he came in. Just made a beeline for the table. Must've just gotten in town, huh?"

Delaney nodded.

"Looks like a real pro to me," Charlie said. "Sure hope he don't skin those boys alive. I kinda depend on their regular business, if you know what I mean."

Delaney nodded again, knowing exactly what the barkeep meant, and knowing as well that Newton's local gamblers were no match for a slick and ruffled dandy like this stranger who claimed to be Ezra Dancer's son.

"I'll keep an eye on him," Delaney said, hoping to reassure Charlie.

"Much obliged, Sheriff." The worried barkeep moved down the bar to draw a beer for another customer.

Keeping an eye out was all he could do right now, Delaney thought. One of the first lessons any lawman learned was that to interrupt men at cards was to risk anger at the very least, a bullet at the worst, especially from the man who was winning. And this Dancer fellow was definitely winning. From Delaney's perspective at the bar, it looked like the stranger was raking in bills and coins manicured hand over ruffled fist.

He wasn't a kid. The man had to be at least thirty, judging from the lines on his face. But Ezra had been in his fifties, so it wasn't out of the question that he could have been married before he'd married Hannah and come to Kansas. Where was it they said he'd lived before? San Francisco?

While he finished his coffee, questions kept forming in Delaney's head. Did Hannah know about this man? Did Ezra's son know he had a beautiful stepmama a few years younger than he?

And then there was the biggest question of all. Why should he even care when he was planning to leave?

The card game lasted until two that afternoon, at which time Dancer emerged from the Wild Horse with his hat at a cocky angle and looking for all the world like a winner. Like a sleek fox who'd just picked the henhouse clean. He gazed up the street, then down the street, as if trying to make up his mind which gambling den to victimize next.

For a moment, his gaze rested on the chair where the sheriff was sitting. The gambler nodded slightly as if in recognition of the badge, as if to say he meant no harm. Delaney responded with a nod of his own, a kind of silent statement that he was keeping an eye on the man and that there best not be any trouble. His right hand flexed instinctively, as if its injured nerves were responding to a crackle of danger in the air.

Even from across the street Delaney could see the man's lips twitch in a smile. Then he turned, walked purposefully along the sidewalk, turned again, and instead of entering another saloon, he began to climb the stairs to Abel Fairfax's office.

So, he had come here to do a little bit more than gamble, after all. As soon as that thought passed through Delaney's mind, he told himself to forget it. Unless it was against the law, it wasn't his business anymore. *She* wasn't his business anymore.

Then, to reinforce that decision, he went into his office, took a sheet of paper from the drawer, and began to compose his letter of resignation. Effective immediately. Today. The hell with waiting around for a qualified replacement.

Chapter Twelve

Hannah stood in the doorway of Ezra's former room, watching Nancy stripping the linens off the bed where the sheriff had slept the night before. She had told the girl to do this immediately after Delaney had walked out the front door. And when Nancy had protested, Hannah had yelled at her. "Now! Do you hear me? Do it now!"

The girl had trudged up the stairs then, and Hannah had followed. Stomping. Furious.

She'd been so angry she'd planned to burn the sheets and pillowcases rather than wash them. Leaving that way. How could he? And after that kiss. That soul-searing kiss that he so cavalierly relegated to the category of goodbye.

But after the linens were all in a jumble in the center of the bare mattress, Hannah's anger waned.

"I'll finish this," she said, motioning Nancy out of the room. "You go back downstairs and see to the rest of breakfast."

The girl sighed. "These're practically clean," she complained. "Shoot. He was only here a couple of nights. Seems to me—"

"That's enough," Hannah snapped. "Close the door on your way out, Nancy."

Left alone, Hannah stared at the rumpled bed. There was no way to tell, now that the linens had been pulled off, whether Delaney had passed a restful night or if he had tossed and turned for hours the way she had. The pillows were at the foot of the bed, which seemed odd, but then Nancy might have put them there in the process of pulling off the sheets. If not, perhaps the man had slept with his head at the foot of the bed, contemptuous of the portrait on the opposite wall, or feeling guilty every time he looked at it, or else—most probably—just ignoring her picture completely.

She gazed around the room, vaguely hoping Delaney had left something behind. A gap-toothed comb perhaps or a threadbare sock. But there was nothing to indicate he'd spent even a single moment here, much less several nights.

Hot tears began to well in Hannah's eyes. She hadn't felt quite this abandoned when Ezra left her. She hadn't felt an overpowering need to seek out his possessions, to savor any object he had touched, to mourn for the lack of a small memento.

Unsteadily, she lowered herself onto the bare mattress and gathered up the bundle of sheets, suffering a keen disappointment when they turned out to be cool rather than warm with Delaney's heat. She buried her face in their folds, needing to breathe in even a hint of his scent. But there was nothing but laundry soap and the faint aroma of eucalyptus that pervaded the whole house.

He was gone, leaving no trace, and it was as if he'd never been here. As if she'd dreamed it all.

But if it had been just a dream, it was over now. Hannah was awake, and her eyes were open wide. "Good riddance," she muttered, punching the linens into a firm bundle.

The house was hers. Delaney had said so. Still, she meant to see to the legalities just in case he changed his mind.

"There's a gent downstairs wants to see you."

Hannah's chin jerked up. Her hands twitched, and the open book on her lap slid to the floor.

"I must have fallen asleep," she said. "What time is it, Nancy?"

"Going on four. What do you want me to tell the gent downstairs?"

"Who is it?"

The girl shrugged. "Dunno. Some slick dandy. Maybe he wants to rent a room."

Hannah stood and smoothed out her skirt, muttering "It'll be a cold day in Hell before I'll let another man into this house."

"So you want me to give him the boot, then?"

"No. I'll see him. Did he give you a name?"

Nancy shook her head.

"All right. Tell him I'll be down in just a moment." Hannah splashed a little water on her face, tended to a few stray wisps of hair and did up the collar button she had loosened earlier.

It wasn't like her to fall asleep in the middle of the afternoon. Her head felt fuzzy now, while her eyes seemed slightly out of focus. She dried her face, then drew in a deep breath and firmed her lips. The last thing she needed was another slick dandy taking up residence in her house, she thought, starting down the stairs.

The man was standing in the vestibule, his back to the stairs, his hat in his hand. Dandy indeed, Hannah thought, as she caught her first glimpse of his fancy suit and ruffled cuffs. His black hair was combed back and it glistened with pomade.

He turned at the sound of her footsteps, giving her a good look at his finely carved features and shockingly blue eyes. There was something so familiar...

"How do you do?" She extended her hand when she reached the bottom of the staircase. "I'm Mrs. Dancer."

He took her hand, shook it politely, then didn't let go when he said, "So you're the little whore my father took up with. Somehow I'd pictured you differently."

Hannah blinked, not certain she'd heard him right, terrified that she had. She tried in vain to pull her hand out of his grasp, but he held her tighter.

"I'm the son. Alec. Or didn't the old man tell you?"

When Hannah failed to reply, he said, "No? I can see from your expression that he failed to mention that. And my mother? Has he failed to mention her, as well?"

For a moment it seemed the stranger was speaking in a foreign language that Hannah only partially understood. The words he spoke had meanings, but taken together, they didn't make sense. She stood here, stupid, speechless.

"Cat got your tongue?"

"No. I…" She didn't know what to say.

"Maybe I'd just better talk to the old man. Where is the bastard, anyway?"

"Where is…?"

"Look, I'm tired of playing games." He slid his hand to her wrist, twisting it. "Now where's my father? Where the stinking hell is he?"

"Let me go. Please." She struggled to free herself. "Ezra's dead."

"He's what?"

"Ezra died three weeks ago. He was ill. He…he killed himself."

"My father's dead?"

Alec Dancer looked stunned, unable to grasp this information. His deep blue eyes kept searching Hannah's face, and it was then she realized that they were Ezra's eyes. Identical in color and shape. And the planes of his face were also the same. She felt as if she were looking at a young Ezra. Ezra ten years before she first met him. There was no question this was his son.

Despite the fact that he was still applying a hurtful pressure on her wrist, she felt a pang of sorrow for him now. After all, he'd just been told his father had passed away.

"I'm sorry," she said.

"You're sorry." His tone was as flat as his expression when he echoed her words. "Sorry," he said again. He let go of her wrist, gave a mournful little sigh and burst out laughing. Then Alec Dancer laughed until tears streamed from his brilliant blue eyes.

Hannah invited the man to stay for supper in spite of the fact that he had called her a whore. Or perhaps she'd extended the invitation to prove to him that she was indeed a proper lady. It was against her better judgment, but she decided it was only right considering that he was Ezra's son.

Ezra's son!

She rocked back and forth in the platform rocker by her bedroom window, having retreated to her room once Alec Dancer had stopped laughing long enough to accept her invitation and after he had made himself quite comfortable with a glass of sherry in the front parlor.

Hannah felt anything but comfortable right now.

She sat with her arms clutched tightly to her chest, her lower lip snagged between her teeth.

Ezra's son! And—great balls of fire—a wife somewhere in California, sometime in his past. In all their fourteen years together, Ezra had never breathed a word about either one of them. Hannah naturally believed he was alone in the world, similar to herself. Why on earth had he deceived her?

She didn't doubt for a moment that it was Ezra who had deceived her, rather than the man who now sat downstairs, sipping sherry and reading the *Weekly Gazette.* The resemblance between the two men was much too striking to be dismissed or denied. He was Ezra's son, no doubt about it. And a son who seemed outrageously pleased to discover that he was now an orphan, perhaps an heir.

Dear God, she wondered, had she been granted a reprieve by Delaney just this morning only to have her house snatched away by this sudden stranger?

Dinner that evening was horrid. Left to her own devices in the kitchen while Hannah stewed and rocked upstairs, Nancy had managed to burn not only the biscuits but the pork chops as well. Her mashed potatoes had lumps the size of small onions in them, only slightly larger than the lumps in the gravy.

When Hannah carried a serving bowl into the dining room from the kitchen, her boarders and her guest were seated at the table. Alec Dancer was ensconced in Ezra's chair at the head of the table and appeared to be paying an almost courtly attention to Florence Green.

From that, Hannah gathered that introductions had already been made. Good, she thought. At least that would spare her making a complete fool of herself. Now she would only seem a partial fool for not knowing about the existence of Ezra's son, not to mention the wife.

When Henry Allen didn't leap to his feet to hold her chair as was his wont, Abel rose from his chair and did the honors.

"Thank you, Abel," Hannah said, settling in at the foot of the table. "Please begin, everyone. I gather you've all met our guest."

There were nods all around, including an especially enthusiastic one from the schoolteacher, who was decked out as gaudily as she had been at breakfast. She and Dancer the Dandy made a perfect pair, Hannah thought uncharitably.

"Where's Delaney?" Abel asked.

"The sheriff left this morning," she said, picking up her fork and trying to sound casual. "He won't be coming back."

Henry made a little snort as if to say good riddance. If Florence even heard, she was far too deep in conversation with Alec to respond to the news about the sheriff. But Abel's expression altered dramatically.

"Oh, my," he said. "Oh, dear." Then he leaned toward Hannah to whisper, "I really must speak with you later this evening. In private. It's rather urgent."

When the old man's gaze flicked ominously toward the head of the table, Hannah's heart sank. And after that she might as well have been eating sawdust for all she tasted of her dinner.

Abel was waiting for her in the parlor after Hannah had dried the glassware that had a tendency to slip out of Nancy's not-so-delicate hands.

"Now what's all this urgency, Abel?" She slid the parlor's pocket doors closed behind her. "Whatever is the matter?"

"Did you know about Ezra's son?"

"No. He never said a word about him." She sat on the sofa beside the old man. "I take it you were just as surprised?"

He nodded. "He came to see me in my office earlier today. I avoided answering any of his questions, Hannah. I didn't even tell him that Ezra was dead. The man's up to no good, I can tell you that."

"I thought as much."

"Still," Abel went on, "I don't think there will be any problem legally. With Ezra's will, I mean. It states in no uncertain terms that Delaney gets this house."

She shook her head. "He doesn't want it."

"What?"

"The sheriff left this morning, Abel. He said he wants nothing further to do with this place." Hannah forced a tiny smile as she smoothed her skirt over her knees. "Or with me either, for that matter."

"Oh, dear." He sat forward a bit, his gray eyebrows knit together in thought. "Delaney plans to relinquish his claim on this property, then?"

"Yes. That was my understanding."

"I see. All right." He seemed to be thinking aloud now, gazing into space rather than at Hannah. "I'll have to look into the legalities, of course, but I don't think that presents any problems. The fact that Ezra didn't leave the house directly to you, I mean."

"Well, Delaney doesn't want it."

"Yes. Yes. I understand. Young Dancer, however, does. He hasn't come right out and said so, but I've concluded that's his plan."

Now it was Hannah's turn to slump forward slightly and to sigh "Oh, dear."

Abel patted her hand. "It's all right, Hannah. Everything will be all right. I'm certain Alec Dancer doesn't stand a chance, my dear. After all, you're Ezra's legal wife. And that's the case we'll make, if it comes to that."

Hannah didn't answer. She couldn't speak. The air in the parlor was suddenly so heavy and oppressive that she could hardly breathe while Abel's words were turning over and over, dizzily, in her head.

That's the case we'll make, if it comes to that.

But Hannah knew only too well, if it came to that, they had no case. They had no case at all.

Chapter Thirteen

Delaney sat watching another sunset, not looking forward to the time when he'd have to go inside the jailhouse and bed down in one of the dank cells. He hadn't even bothered confronting Alma Spence again about a room at the National, figuring he could tolerate a night or two on a pancake-flat mattress in his office.

His letter of resignation was still locked away in the top drawer of his desk. What a sorry document that had turned out to be, penned with his bad right hand. He was almost ashamed to have anybody read it with its crabbed, shaky letters, like those of a doddering, half-blind old man. His days of penmanship awards were far behind him, he thought bleakly, along with prizes and applause for marksmanship.

"Vanity," he muttered with some disgust. But it wasn't that and he damn well knew it. That bullet last year had robbed him of a sense of wholeness that had nothing to do with being vain. It was about being a man. It was as simple as that, and as complicated. He was used to being in control, whether that meant using a pistol or putting down legible words on a page.

Those abilities seemed out of his feeble grasp now. Oh, sure. He could still do considerable damage with a shotgun and he could still sign his name even if it did look like the signature of an arthritic old coot. He'd even mastered—sort of—buttoning his clothes with his left hand when his right hand failed him. But being adequate had never been Delaney's style, dammit. He was used to being the best.

Hannah. Her name played in his mind like an old, familiar tune. He wished he'd never met her. Or wished he'd met her when he was a better man. A whole one. Before he was damaged goods.

He sighed. Then, in an attempt to erase the woman from his mind, he tried to put names to the people who passed by on the street, the men and women out for an evening stroll, or going in and out of various doors for a variety of purposes.

Sam Kennett came out of the pharmacy, locked the door behind him, tried it once as he always did to make sure the lock held, then headed for the Wild Horse saloon, where Delaney knew the cautious man would have a single beer before walking home.

Old humpbacked Ada Murphy came out of a side door of the National, where she'd worked all day under the beady eyes and bullwhip tongue of Alma Spence. Now Ada would go home to clean and cook supper for her good-for-nothing husband, Ed.

Young Dick Hutchins rode by on his newly broken Appaloosa mare. He'd purchased her the week before in Dodge. "Evening, Sheriff," he called.

"How's the horse?" Delayed inquired.

"Taking the bit real good. Real good. Thanks for asking."

The street got quiet again. The dust settled. And Delaney couldn't help but think how much he had come to like Newton and its citizens, who were friendly and hardworking for the most part. He hadn't planned to care about the town at all, considering it merely a way station between Dodge City and Tombstone, regarding it only as a place to heal between dangerous jobs.

But he hadn't really healed, had he? Not enough, anyway. And Newton, this way station, had started to feel a lot more like home than any place he'd been in the last several years.

"I wonder if I might have a word with you, Sheriff?"

Delaney had been so lost in thought he hadn't noticed Abel Fairfax approach him. Now that the man stood beside him, he couldn't help but notice the worried look on his usually placid face. His brow was deeply furrowed and his mouth drooped like a tattered flag.

"Have a seat, Abel." He motioned behind him. "Pull up that chair."

After the older man sat down with a mighty sigh, Delaney asked him, "Something on your mind?"

"Something," he muttered as he folded his hands over his belly. "This isn't working out the way it was supposed to. None of it."

Delaney hadn't the least notion what Abel was talking about, but he figured the man would get to the point eventually. In the meantime, he didn't mind a little quiet conversation to distract him from his own sorry problems. Hell, he welcomed it.

"Hannah tells me you've walked out on your inheritance. That you don't want the house."

"That's right."

Abel sat in silence a moment, as if mulling over Delaney's terse reply. As if there were something to mull over. There wasn't, though. No meant no as far as Delaney was concerned.

"Why not?"

Abel's question took him by surprise. It wasn't the one Delaney had expected. Nor one he could answer truthfully without sounding like five kinds of fool. He felt a muscle jerk in his cheek.

"I'm leaving town," he said. "For Arizona. No use having my name on that house if I'm not here to be responsible. And if I sold it…" He squinted into the sunset and forced a small grin. "Well, hell, Abel. What's the point? I'd just waste the money anyway."

"You don't give yourself much credit, son," the older man said softly.

"Maybe not," Delaney agreed.

"Ezra thought quite highly of you. So do all the folks here in town."

"Yeah, well..."

"Being held in high regard isn't something to be sneered at. And it isn't something to just walk away from, either. Not in my opinion anyway."

Delaney continued to gaze west. In silence.

"You'd probably prefer I kept my opinions to myself, I guess." Abel chuckled for a moment and then his tone grew serious again. "I can't do that. Not in this case anyhow. I owe it to my friend Ezra to see that Hannah doesn't lose that house."

"I told her..."

"I know what you told her. That you're relinquishing your claim. But that doesn't make much difference now."

Delaney let the sunset go and turned his gaze on the man beside him. "Why's that?"

"Do you know who's shown up in town?"

"The son?"

Abel nodded.

"I don't see what difference that makes. Are you thinking he'll press a claim?"

The old man nodded again. "I'd be willing to bet my life on it. He didn't know his father was dead. His mother passed away this spring after he'd milked her of every last penny Ezra settled on her. So he came looking for Ezra. Looking for money to pay some gambling debts he owes. Big ones. Big enough to be worth his life."

"He told you all this?"

"In a roundabout way. He came to see me, trying

to get a proper fix on his dad's worldly goods and such before he went fortune hunting. I didn't tell him much. But now he knows that Ezra's dead and those worldly goods are up for grabs, at least in Alec Dancer's opinion.''

''I don't see how that affects my giving up the house. Ezra may have left it to me, but Hannah's his widow after all.''

''Ah,'' Abel interrupted him. ''There's the rub.''

''What do you mean?''

''Hannah. You see, she isn't his widow. She never was his wife.''

That was the kind of news that kept a man staring at the ceiling all night long. In Delaney's case, the ceiling was a cracked and peeling stucco above the rickety cot in a cell. He'd left a lamp burning on his desk, and it cast strange, disproportioned shadows on the jailhouse walls.

She never was his wife.

Abel hadn't said much more than that before they were interrupted by a shout and then the wild hoofbeats of Dick Hutchins's Appaloosa, racing riderless down the center of Main Street. Delaney had had to chase the mare all the way out to Beech Creek before he caught her dangling reins. By the time he'd led the reluctant animal back to town, it was dark and Abel Fairfax had disappeared.

She never was his wife.

For lack of a pillow Delaney hooked his arms behind his head. It was hard thinking of Hannah as Ezra's mistress after spending such a long time avoiding her because he thought she was Ezra's wife. It was nearly impossible to regard her as the sort of woman who'd live with a man outside the blessings and legal bonds of matrimony.

Not that he held that against her. He knew plenty of good women—Wyatt's Mattie and Doc's Kate, to name just two—who weren't married to their men for one reason or another. Even so, Ezra hadn't struck him as the sort of man who'd fail to make an honest woman of his companion. Especially a woman like Hannah.

He sighed roughly as he turned on his side, trying to fall into the oblivion of sleep. Whatever he thought about Hannah or her circumstances, past or present, didn't really matter. As for her future...well...he wouldn't be around to see it, would he?

When the clock in the vestibule struck midnight, Hannah bolted upright in bed.

"Do something," she said out loud. "You have to do *something*."

But what?

She flopped back down, her mind empty of everything but worry, her heart so full of fear that it seemed to be actually pressing her deeper and deeper into the mattress.

It was useless at this point to be furious with Ezra for his deceit and for the precarious position he'd put her in. Deep down, Hannah knew he hadn't done any of it with malice, but whatever had been going on in that head of his, she was certain she didn't know.

What she did know, though, was that worrying didn't solve problems. And if she just lay in bed and worried, she'd find herself out on the street sooner or later without even a bed to worry in. She'd been homeless fourteen years ago and it wasn't something she ever wanted to be again. Not if she could help it. And maybe, just maybe, she could.

Please let him still be in town, she prayed.

She kicked back the covers and nearly vaulted out of bed. Then, without lighting the lamp, she struggled into the clothes she'd taken off earlier, slipped on her shoes, gave her hair a quick, hard brushing, and tiptoed out into the hall.

It wasn't until she had tiptoed halfway down the dark staircase that Hannah realized there was somebody tiptoeing *up.*

"Good lord, Florence! You nearly scared me to death. Whatever are you doing up at this hour of the night?"

"Is it so very late?" the schoolteacher whispered.

"After midnight."

"My stars!" Florence giggled behind her hand. "I had no idea."

Even in the darkness, Hannah could see that the young woman's balance left a bit to be desired. And, if she wasn't mistaken, there was the faintest trace of liquor on her breath.

"I was out promenading with Alec," she said. "We had such a lovely time."

"Promenading? All this while?"

"Well..." Florence giggled again. "We did stop for a bit of refreshment, I must admit."

Hannah hoped that was all they had stopped for, and she very nearly said so until she reminded herself that Florence Green was over twenty-one and entitled to make her own mistakes if she so chose. The silly, fickle girl. It hadn't taken her long to transfer her affections from the sheriff to the slick-combed dandy, had it? Hannah thought with some disgust.

"Well, do hold on to the bannister, Florence. I don't want you toppling down the staircase and breaking all your bones."

Hannah squeezed past the tipsy schoolteacher and continued down the stairs.

"Good night, Mrs. Dancer." Florence sighed. "Such a beautiful name. Mrs. Dancer. Why it's almost like a lovely tune. Aren't you fortunate?" She gave another moist little sigh then and wobbled up the stairs.

Heading out the front door, Hannah felt neither fortunate nor blessed with a beautiful name. She wasn't Mrs. Dancer. She never had been. Ezra merely lent her his name.

She walked down her long brick path, through the deep, moon-cast shadows of elms. The night was still warm, and a small breeze riffled her unbound hair. Locusts sang high over her head and crickets chirped at her feet. For a moment Hannah found herself envying Florence her promenade on such a lovely summer night, and wondered if she herself would ever again stroll with her hand poised delicately on the strong, warm arm of a man.

How she missed that, she thought. But that was the least of her problems right now. If she didn't do something about her current situation, she'd soon find herself missing a lot more than an escorted evening stroll. So she quickened her pace along the street, her eyes locked on her destination—the sheriff's office, where a soft light glowed through the window even at this late hour.

At first Delaney ignored the soft knock on the door. If there were trouble, the rapping would increase and then he'd get up and do his job. But if it was just somebody up late, looking for a little conversation to while away the long and lonely hours of the night, he didn't want any part of it. He shifted onto his left side, his back turned to the door.

The knocking came again, this time a little more persistent. And then he heard Hannah's voice.

"Delaney? Are you in there?"

He wished he weren't. He wished he were anyplace else but here, where the woman he wanted so fiercely was just outside his door. After midnight. Knocking. What in blazes did she want?

He shouldered off the mattress and sat up while the knocking continued. "Just a minute," he called, rubbing his eyes, running his fingers through his hair, and muttering curses all the while.

"Door's open," he called out. "Quit knocking, Hannah. Just walk the hell in."

Actually he was hoping his intentional rudeness would make her angry enough to curse him and walk away, but no such luck. The knob turned slowly and the door pushed in a few inches.

"Delaney?"

"Yeah," he grumbled.

The door moved a few more inches.

"Well, come in if you're coming." He sounded like a grizzly being rousted from a long winter's nap. "Come on," he added a bit more hospitably.

Then she was inside, and lamplight burnished her long and unbound hair, making it look like fire spilling over her shoulders. Delaney's heart instantly became a hard fist in his chest.

"I woke you," she said. "I'm sorry."

"That's all right." Damned if he'd tell her he hadn't been sleeping because his brain was so full of her there was no room left over for sleep.

He stood up, walked out of the cell toward his desk, where he propped a hip on the corner and folded his arms. He could almost feel the scowl on his face smooth out as he looked at her pretty face. How long could a man, a mere mortal, withstand the sheer beauty of a redheaded angel? he wondered.

"It's late," he said quietly. "You shouldn't be out all by yourself."

She stood there, staring at the floor, chewing on her lower lip so long he didn't think she'd ever speak. Then finally she lifted her eyes to his. "Help me, Delaney. Please."

"Help you?" He gave a bitter little laugh. "Lady, I can't even help myself."

"Have you heard that Ezra's son has shown up in town?"

"I heard."

"He's here for only one reason. Money. He was hoping to borrow whatever he could from his father. But now, with Ezra gone, I'm convinced he'll try to get the house."

Delaney knew all that and more, but he was curious to see if Hannah, in her desperation, would tell him the whole truth, or if her pride would prevail and she'd rather lose her house than admit she'd lived with Ezra out of wedlock.

"I have a hard time picturing any court of law picking a derelict son over a widow," he said. "I wouldn't worry if I were you."

She consulted the floor again and gnawed on her bottom lip. "You don't understand." Her voice sounded small as a child's.

"No, I guess I don't."

He was testing her, Delaney realized all of a sudden. Testing this woman cruelly for his own sake. He was goading her to lie to him so he could feel justified and free of guilt when he told her no, he wouldn't help. He was done with this. Her.

"Well, it isn't easy to explain."

"Try," he told her. What he meant was go ahead and lie.

Hannah met his gaze then and spoke slowly. "Ezra and I were together for fourteen years. I used his name, Delaney. But we…" She cleared her throat as if the words had gotten stuck there. "We were never married. I'm not his widow. Does that shock you?"

What shocked him was that she had told the truth, that this beautiful woman had just put her reputation in his hands. Did she trust him that much? Or was it simply a measure of her desperation?

"Shock me?" He shook his head. "No. But I'll admit I never would have guessed. You played your part pretty well. Ezra, too."

"Yes, I suppose we did."

"Who was it didn't want to tie the knot?" he asked.

"Ezra. Of course, I never suspected it was because he already had a wife in California. I thought it was because—"

Hannah stopped in the middle of her sentence, tightening her lips. She'd said far too much already, she decided. Delaney didn't need to know all of the intimate details of her relationship with Ezra.

Then it suddenly occurred to her that it was better—perfect, in fact—if he assumed she was a fallen woman who'd long been living in sin. That notion—that aura of sexual abandon—just might make her more attractive to him.

And now Hannah wanted him to desire her desperately, to need to do far more than merely kiss her.

She'd come here tonight not knowing exactly what she was going to say or how she was going to enlist the sheriff's aid. Now all of a sudden she knew. It hit her like a bolt of lightning. She stepped closer to where he sat on the corner of his desk.

"Marry me, Delaney," she said. "I'll make it worth your while."

Chapter Fourteen

Delaney laughed. He couldn't help himself, then immediately apologized when Hannah's pretty mouth curved down at the corners and her green eyes glistened with tears.

"I'm sorry. Judas!" he exclaimed. "You just took me by surprise."

She stiffened a little, her lips firming and her chin going up one or two notches. "Is it so outlandish? Our marrying?"

"To keep a house away from a greedy, good-for-nothing gambler? Yeah." He nodded. "That strikes me as pretty outlandish, Hannah, if you want to know the truth. I've heard of a lot of reasons for marrying, but that sure isn't one of them."

"And the notion of being married to me has absolutely no appeal?" she asked at the same time that she stepped a bit closer to him.

She stood close enough now that Delaney could feel her leg pressing through her skirt against his thigh. It was distracting as hell so he shifted his weight a bit, decreasing the contact.

"The notion of being married to anybody doesn't have much appeal," he said. "I'm not that kind of man."

"Oh. And just what kind of man are you, Delaney?"

"Not the kind you want. Or need. Believe me." He said it almost harshly because he didn't trust the way he was feeling just then. As if there was nothing more in the world he wanted than to be with this woman, to claim her in every way a man claimed a woman. But it was true, what he'd told her. He wasn't what she thought she wanted or needed. He couldn't be.

"It's very presumptuous of you, Sheriff, thinking you know exactly what I want or what I need." It was Hannah's turn to laugh softly now. She shook her head. "I'm not even sure I know those things myself. But I do know we could work out some sort of arrangement, you and I. One that would certainly benefit us both."

Delaney cocked his head and met her bold gaze. "That's a long way to go for a piece of property, Hannah. Trading yourself for—what?—ten or twelve rooms and an acre of clipped grass."

"You needn't make it sound so...so cold and calculating," she said indignantly.

"Isn't it?"

"Well, no. No, it's not." She sighed then as she searched for a word. "It's…well…it's a plan."

"A plan," Delaney echoed. "Why don't you plan to marry the gambler?"

"Marry Alec Dancer? That's absurd."

"I don't know why."

"Because I don't lo—" She stopped short, looking startled if not downright shocked. Her hand fluttered up to her mouth and she blinked. "What I meant to say was…"

Delaney had no idea what she'd meant to say, but he knew that what she did say, at least halfway, was "Because I don't love him." Nobody had been talking about love, he thought, unless he had completely misunderstood their conversation. That was a distinct possibility, though, considering what this woman did to his brain.

"I really should be going." Hannah was turning toward the door even as she spoke, practically running away from him then. Her black skirts rustled furiously.

"I'll walk you home."

"No. Please. I'm sorry I woke you. Good night."

She went through the door as if she were escaping a burning building, and the last thing Delaney saw was a wisp of dark petticoat when she picked up her skirts and ran.

Out of breath when she reached her front door, Hannah collapsed in a heap of black silk on the porch while her mind continued to race.

What had she almost said in the sheriff's office? That she loved him? No. She recalled her words clearly. She'd started to say she wouldn't marry Alec Dancer "because I don't love him."

She'd meant that. But the clear implication—the one that had stunned her like a bolt from the heavens—was that she loved Delaney instead.

Love him! Why, it had never crossed her mind. Love him! She hardly knew Delaney. God almighty! She didn't even know the man's Christian name. All this worrying about the house had made her a little bit crazy. As loony as a fruitcake. As daft as a March hare. Or maybe it was too much night air that made her so susceptible to such strange notions.

Love indeed!

Hannah struggled up from the porchboards. "Well, you made a mess of that," she grumbled, brushing dust from her dress, wondering just how she was going to set the sheriff straight on her exact feelings.

Well, she would. She had to. Just as soon as she figured out what those exact feelings were.

The next morning, though, Hannah hadn't figured out a thing when Delaney showed up bright and early at the back door.

"You left this behind last night," he said, holding out her black satin reticule, letting it dangle casually from his hand.

Hannah opened the screen door a fraction and snatched the purse. "Thank you."

"About last night, Hannah…"

She tried to close the door, but Delaney had too good a grip on it with his left hand. They played tug-of-war for a moment.

"I'd rather not discuss it," she said with a hiss, exerting all her strength on the metal door handle. "Not now."

"I guess you did all your talking last night, huh?" He pulled a little harder on the door. "Let me in, Hannah. It's time for me to do some talking of my own."

Hannah didn't budge and wouldn't let go of the door. It was Nancy who finally resolved their standoff when she came up behind Hannah with a pan of dirty dishwater and said, "'Scuse me. I need to throw this out."

Sighing, Hannah let go of the door and stepped out of the girl's way. At the same time, Delaney got out of her line of fire. Nancy flung the water sideways, over the flowerbed, and when she stepped back inside, the sheriff was right on her heels.

"Give me five minutes, Hannah. That's all I ask."

"Oh, all right," she snapped. "Follow me."

Then, without waiting for his reply, she turned and left the kitchen for the front parlor and some small measure of privacy. She didn't have the foggiest notion what Delaney intended to say, but she was certain she didn't want everybody in the house to hear it. Whatever it was.

She lowered herself onto the horsehair sofa and sat primly, her hands folded in her lap, awaiting him. For a man so desperate to talk, he was certainly taking his time!

Then, suddenly he was there, in the doorway where he had kissed her the night before last. Hannah felt a hot flush creep up her neck and flare across her cheeks at the mere memory. Her heart began to beat a little faster while she watched Delaney close the pocket doors behind him.

He stood there a moment, just looking at her. It was only then that Hannah realized how tired the sheriff appeared. His autumn-colored eyes seemed a bit more hazy than usual, and there were a few lines in his handsome face that she had never noticed before. She could tell that he had shaved just recently, nicking his chin in the process.

"You look tired," she said quietly. She patted the sofa seat. "Come. Sit down."

"I am tired," he said, offering her a weak grin. "You have a way of making it hard for a man to get back to sleep."

"I'm sorry, Delaney. It was a half-baked idea, anyway. I really hadn't thought it through."

"Well, I did." He lowered himself beside her on the sofa and planted his hat on his knee. "Last night, since I wasn't sleeping, I thought it all through. Hell,

I thought it sideways, and inside out, and even upside down.''

Hannah raised her eyebrows. ''And did you come to any conclusions?''

''One,'' he answered.

When he didn't continue, she tilted her head and asked, ''Are you going to tell me what you concluded or am I supposed to guess?''

''I was going to leave, Hannah. Today. I had even written out my letter of resignation for the mayor and the town council, but I tore it up this morning.'' He sighed, giving his hat a quarter turn. ''Look. I'll stay. Just long enough to make sure you keep your house.''

''I'm very grateful.''

Grateful! she thought. She was more than grateful. She was wild with relief. Beside herself with joy. Without even thinking, she threw her arms around the sheriff and kissed him full on the mouth.

He pulled away as if her lips had burned him. His voice was stern, almost harsh, when he said, ''It's not going to be like that, Hannah. Us, I mean. You and me.''

She was too elated that moment to feel rejected. ''I was only thanking you.''

''Well, just say it then. No kissing. All right?''

Hannah laughed. ''I promise. No kissing. Thank you, Delaney. Thank you a million times.''

''You're welcome,'' he said through clenched teeth. But then he appeared to relax ever so slightly as he continued to speak. ''What I'll do is move back in here, let Dancer see that I'm staking my claim on my inheritance. If we're lucky, he'll just drift out of town and find his fortune someplace else.''

"And if we're not lucky?" she asked.

He frowned while one finger traced the leather band on his hat. ''Then we'll just have to wait and see what sort of hand he tries to play.''

Hannah nodded in understanding. ''I'd be willing to bet he's got more than one ace up his sleeve, too.''

''I wouldn't bet against it.'' He stood up. ''All right, then. I'll move back in tonight.''

When Hannah rose, he backed a step away from her. ''I'll have Nancy get your room ready,'' she said.

''Fine.'' He started toward the door. ''Oh, and one more thing. No more talk about marriage or any of those arrangements. I'll stay till the house is clearly yours, and then I'll be leaving for Arizona. That's the way it has to be, Hannah. Do you understand?''

She nodded as if she did, when in fact she didn't understand at all why Delaney was making such a big issue of her misguided proposal the night before.

''Good,'' he said. ''I'll see you later.''

Just as he was going out the door, Hannah called out, ''Delaney! Wait!''

He turned back. ''What?''

''I want to ask you something. Something that's been bothering me.''

He raised an eyebrow. ''What's that?''

''I don't even know your Christian name, Delaney. What the devil is it, anyway?''

"I never use it."

"Still—"

He interrupted her, his voice a notch lower than normal, his tone almost threatening. "Don't get close, Hannah. I told you. Don't even try."

"I wasn't."

"Good."

And then he was gone.

After spending the next three nights in the bedroom adjacent to Hannah's, Delaney was more exhausted than he'd ever been in his life. Even during the war, he'd always managed to fall asleep the minute he closed his eyes despite any racket going on around him.

Not that the Dancer house was noisy. Just the opposite, in fact. The place was so quiet he kept imagining that he could hear Hannah breathing in the room next door to his or rustling the bedclothes when she turned over in her sleep. He lay there every night, his head always at the foot of the bed, ignoring her portrait, listening to the clock downstairs in the vestibule as it counted off the hours.

Each night, not long after twelve, he'd hear the schoolteacher and the gambler say good-night on the porch below his open window. Then, like clockwork, he'd listen to Florence Green's tipsy tread coming up the stairs and going down the hallway to her room. Dancer's footsteps always headed back in the direction of the saloons.

The gambler slept all day, apparently, then played cards most of the night. Delaney rarely saw him, and he didn't know if that was intentional on Dancer's part or not. But the man seemed to be behaving himself. Delaney had made a couple inquiries. Nobody had any complaints. Not yet, anyway.

The chubby schoolmarm certainly wasn't complaining. She seemed besotted with Alec Dancer, much to the consternation of young Henry Allen. The more Florence Green disdained him these days, the more the banker adored her. The young man who'd once been so sweet on Hannah appeared totally oblivious of her now. Which was fine with Delaney. Even though he had no romantic intentions himself, he didn't particularly enjoy watching anybody else make eyes at Hannah.

He let out his breath in a weary sigh, then sat up and reached for his watch on the bedside table. It agreed with the clock downstairs, informing him this was the third night in a row he'd been wide awake past one o'clock. Sighing again, he exchanged the watch for a small, tight ball of twine, then lay back down and began to squeeze the object again and again with his right hand.

It was therapy of his own design. There was just the slightest give in the twine, allowing him to compress it. He couldn't be sure, but he thought his hand felt a little stronger than it did the week before.

Hell, if nothing else, he thought, it was a way to pass the time until daylight.

Delaney and Abel Fairfax were the first ones down to breakfast the following morning.

"You're looking a little peaked, Sheriff," Abel said, gazing over a turned-down corner of his newspaper.

"Nothing a few good hours of sleep won't cure," Delaney answered.

Abel folded his paper and put it down. "I haven't had an opportunity to thank you for what you're doing for Hannah. Ezra would be most grateful. I hope you realize that."

"It doesn't matter," Delaney said, leaning back while Nancy filled his cup with hot coffee. More often than not he thought the not-so-graceful girl was going to dump the whole pot in his lap. "Thanks," he said when she was finished.

After Nancy had returned to the kitchen, Abel began talking again, his voice fairly low as if he didn't want anyone to overhear.

"I'm curious, Delaney. Have you got this all figured out yet?"

"All what?"

"Hannah. The house. You. The prodigal son."

The sheriff shook his head. "What's to figure? Seems to me Ezra was just doing his best to take care of her after he was gone. Especially since he knew damn well he had legal heirs he'd abandoned along the way."

When Abel nodded and gave him a knowing little smile, Delaney continued.

"That business in his will about my saving his life back in January was just a crock of bull."

It was a statement, not a question, but when the older man grinned a little and his eyes started to twinkle, Delaney knew his suspicions were right on target.

"That old fox didn't set me up to inherit his house. He appointed me the protector of his wife." He muttered a soft curse, then corrected himself. "His woman, I mean."

"It's true," Abel said, not looking the least bit surprised. "That was the only way Ezra felt he could do right by Hannah."

"He might have consulted me."

"You'd have said no."

"Damn right."

"Well, then." Abel laughed. "Ezra knew what he was doing. You're here, aren't you? Protecting her."

But the sheriff didn't laugh in return. Instead, he scowled and aimed a dark, hard glare across the table. "I'm here," he said. "For now."

"Ezra was pretty sure you would be. He hoped…no, he *believed* that you would stay. And not just for a while. But for good. That's why he chose you."

"For good? Now why the hell would that old codger think anything of the kind?"

"Do you really want to know the answer to that?" Abel raised one thick gray eyebrow.

"I wouldn't ask if I didn't want an answer."

"No, I suppose not." The older man leaned a bit

toward Delaney across the table. He spoke in an even lower, more secretive voice. "When he was making out his will, Ezra confided in me that there were...well...feelings, strong ones, between you and Hannah. From the very beginning, he told me, it had been obvious to him."

Judas, Delaney thought. Had he been so easy—he and Hannah, both—for that old man to read? He felt more than a little ashamed of himself now for those feelings. If he'd been Ezra, he'd have shot the randy new sheriff dead. But Ezra had shot himself instead, and handed his house as well as his woman into the sheriff's care.

"Does Hannah know about this?" he asked the older man.

Before he got an answer, however, a bright voice sounded at his back.

"Does Hannah know about what?"

She startled him so that Delaney's right hand automatically dropped to his right hip for the pistol that, of course, wasn't there. Across the table, Abel Fairfax—the coward!—disappeared behind his newspaper.

"Does Hannah know about what?" she repeated, taking her seat at the foot of the table.

"Nothing." Delaney shot to his feet the instant Hannah sat down. "I'm late for work."

As he headed out the door, he heard her repeat her question to Abel. Then he heard the man's calm reply.

"He wondered if you knew this morning's cream for the coffee was a bit off."

"Is it?" he heard Hannah say. "Nancy is supposed to check these things. I'll have a word with her."

Once the front door closed behind him, Delaney heard nothing more. But crafty old Abel hadn't answered his question, had he? Just how much of Ezra's plan did Hannah really know? Or—the thought hit him with the force of a vicious slap across his cheek—was it Hannah's plan from the very start?

Chapter Fifteen

"This cream ain't off." Nancy's nose jerked up from the little porcelain pitcher, her plain face registering self-righteousness and pained indignance. "Here, Miz Dancer." She slid the pitcher across the table. "You take a whiff of it yourself."

Hannah did, and decided she completely agreed with the poor girl. The cream was fine. But something wasn't. Delaney and Abel had been conspiring in the dining room this morning. She was sure of it now.

"Nancy," she asked as casually as she could, "Did you happen to hear any of the conversation this morning between Mr. Fairfax and the sheriff?"

"No, ma'am, I didn't." The girl's chapped lips thinned in a stubborn line. "You told me I wasn't to be listening in where it don't concern me, remember? Told me more than once, too."

"I wasn't accusing you of eavesdropping, for heaven's sake," Hannah insisted. There were times when Nancy's hard-won lessons were a kind of victory, but this wasn't one of them.

She sighed, attempting to soften her tone a bit so as not to seem threatening or accusatory. "I know you just happen to stand at the dining room door now and then while you're doing up the dishes. I only wondered if you might have heard my name mentioned this morning by those two gentlemen before I came downstairs. That's all."

Nancy's eyes narrowed in suspicion, as if she might be walking into a lethal trap or just plain talking herself out of employment.

"Well, I did hear a name," she said, "but it wasn't yours. I was just passing by the door, minding my own business, when I happened to hear them say Mr. Dancer's name a time or two."

"Which Mr. Dancer?" Hannah asked immediately.

"Why, yours, ma'am. Mr. Ezra."

"And while you were just passing by the door did you happen to hear what they said about Mr. Dancer?"

The girl's eyes narrowed even more, causing Hannah to exclaim, "I'm not going to punish you, you silly girl. Now tell me what they said, if you heard anything."

"Something about Mr. Ezra planning it without never asking the sheriff," Nancy whined. "And something about his staying on here for good."

"Who staying on here?"

"The sheriff."

"Anything else?"

The girl shrugged. "That's all I heard. Honest it was." She crossed her heart, twice, on top of her grimy apron. "And none of it made a nickel's worth of sense to me, anyways."

Hannah wasn't sure it made a nickel's worth of sense to her, either. But she turned Nancy's words over and over in her brain all that day. While she was tending the vegetable garden. While she washed the rich dirt off her hands, and later when she manicured her ragged nails. She thought about those words when she peered out her bedroom window, down the street, hoping for a glimpse of the sheriff in his chair.

If she did see him, she thought, she might be tempted to walk the short distance to his office and ask him exactly what his conversation with Abel was about. What blasted plan of Ezra's? What the devil was going on?

She didn't see him, though, despite the fact that she peeked out her window at least a dozen times. Delaney didn't come home for the evening meal, either.

By the time Hannah climbed into bed, she was determined to stay awake until he came home. She wanted answers, and she wanted them tonight.

Delaney had returned home deliberately late, barely making it up the stairs before the schoolteacher arrived and began her customary wobble up to her room. He listened to her passage down the hall before he took off all but his union suit, then stretched out on the bed, dreading the long, almost endless hours until morning.

He'd thought about Ezra Dancer all day. Most of his thoughts were colored dark with regret and guilt. He wished he'd never come to Newton. He wished he'd never coveted another man's woman. Of all the commandments he'd broken in his years, "Thou shalt not covet they neighbor's wife" struck him as the worst, the most shameful, and the one that would surely earn him his rightful place in hell.

He felt like a fool, too, having been manipulated by a man's last will and testament. If what Abel Fairfax had told him was true, then Ezra had played him like a fine violin. Or Hannah had. Delaney still didn't know who had been the author of the plan, the spinner of the web he found himself caught in.

Maybe it didn't matter who had trapped him, he thought now. Trapped was trapped regardless of the cause.

There was a soft knock on his door, followed by Hannah's whispered, "Delaney?"

He closed his eyes. He didn't answer, but just lay there trying to keep his breathing even and deep.

"Delaney?"

She tried the door, jiggling the knob and quickly discovering it was locked.

"Delaney, please."

He imagined her—pale hand still curled around the brass knob, her smooth forehead pressed lightly to the door, and her red hair spilling forward over her shoulders and breasts like liquid fire—and still he didn't answer.

A moment later there came a small creak in one of the floorboards in the hall and then the sound of Hannah's door clicking closed. Delaney let out a long breath, only to suck it in again when the dressing room door—the one connecting Hannah's room to Ezra's—slid open. He didn't need to look. He could feel her standing there even before she spoke.

"I tried to stay awake until you got home, but I guess I fell asleep. I need to speak with you. It's imperative. Otherwise... Well, it can't wait."

"Not even a couple of hours till morning?"

"No."

He sighed and sat up, leaning to light the lamp beside the bed.

"No, don't," she said. "I'd rather it were dark."

"All right." He put down the box of matches then sat with his arms braced on his knees.

What he wanted to tell her was "Get out of my bedroom, Hannah. You're only asking for trouble here." But even without the lamp lit, he could see her hair flowing over the shoulders of her pale satin robe and her slippers peeking from beneath her hem, making her seem as vulnerable as a child. That appearance of innocence and vulnerability led him to infuse a note of patience in his voice.

"What's so important that it can't wait until the morning?"

"I need to know what you and Abel were discussing this morning at the breakfast table."

"Nothing," he said. "Nothing important."

"Maybe not to you, Delaney, but it's important to me. What's all this business about a plan Ezra had? And why must it be a secret from me? I feel…" Her voice wavered. "I feel foolish. And used, too. Like some silly and empty-headed puppet left dancing on invisible strings."

He stared at her in the darkness. She was wringing her hands. "So it wasn't your plan, then," he murmured.

"What plan?" Hannah raised those hands in frustration, now, raising her voice a notch as well. "What confounded plan?"

"Hush." He smoothed the bedcovers and patted the mattress beside him. "Come over here and sit. You don't want the whole house hearing this."

She stood there a moment, swaying a bit, seemingly reluctant to move until Delaney held out his hand.

"Come on," he said. "It's all right."

The satin of her gown and robe swished as she came forward, feminine sounds that nearly had Delaney regretting his impulsive invitation. When she sat, her floral fragrance enveloped him, even though she positioned herself a pristine several inches away. After breathing in her aura, he added a little distance of his own by shifting farther onto his right hip.

"What is it you need to know?" he asked.

"This plan..." she began. "I don't understand it at all. What was Ezra up to?"

"I don't know, Hannah." He let out a weary sigh that felt as if it came from the soles of his feet. "It looks to me like Ezra had an idea how he wanted things to be after he was dead. Mostly how he wanted to make certain you were taken care of."

"I had figured most of that out on my own," she said, folding her hands in her lap, lacing her fingers together. "I mean, I assumed he left the house to you just in case his wayward son ever happened to show up and cause trouble."

"Yeah. That was probably a good part of it," he agreed.

"A good part? What more could Ezra have intended?"

Delaney didn't answer right away. She was entitled to the truth—all of it—he knew, but this particular truth was going to lead them into dangerous territory. He wasn't at all sure he wanted to go there.

"Delaney?"

Well, hell. They were both grown-ups, people who knew how to control their feelings and urges. God knows they'd done it in the past. Hannah's knowing the truth wouldn't make it any different.

"Ezra knew," he said, "And don't ask me how. But he knew you and I had feelings for each other. That there was a pull there. An attraction between you and me."

She gave a little gasp. "There wasn't. I never... I swear."

"Hannah. He knew. He damn well knew."

Then it was her turn to lapse into silence with her hands clenched in her lap and her head bowed. She rocked back and forth a little before she lifted her head and said, "It was wrong of me. I tried so hard to pretend those feelings didn't exist. And...and..." She laughed softly, bleakly. "And all the while Ezra knew. He knew! Oh, I'm so ashamed."

She started to get up then, to flee, but he caught her hand and pulled her back down. There was no sense now not telling her the rest of it. At least as far as he understood Ezra's crazy plan.

"He figured those feelings would one day lead us down the aisle. I guess he thought you'd be safe with me. Taken care of. Hell, I don't know." He lifted his shoulders in a shrug. "Maybe even happy."

She turned her face to his then, looking so beautiful despite the dark that he felt his heart take an extra and unbidden beat inside his chest.

"And was he so terribly wrong?" she whispered.

It was all Delaney could do to keep himself planted on the mattress when his every instinct told him to get up and get out and then get as far away as possible.

"Hannah," he murmured, his voice betraying his confusion more than he wanted. Then he just shook his head, not knowing what else to say, unable to move for the seizing up of his heart, the unreliability of his breathing, and the heavy, molten flow of blood southward in his body.

"I do feel safe with you, Delaney. Why shouldn't we...why couldn't we be happy?" She slid her hand into his, not letting him pull away. "I do have those feelings Ezra somehow sensed or recognized. Even more feelings now. They're burning me up, Delaney. Ever since you kissed me..."

"Judas! Hannah, don't."

"What? Don't admit that Ezra was right? Or..." She leaned against him, her cheek pressed to his shoulder. "Don't ask you to kiss me again? The way you did the other night?"

"That was a mistake." The gruffness he intended sounded more like huskiness, though. *What are you doing, you damn fool?* Delaney asked himself. *Why not give her what she wants? And more. Make her want more. God knows you do.*

"Liar," she breathed against his ear. "That kiss was no mistake. And it wasn't goodbye, either. It was hello." Her lips brushed his ear, his cheek. "Do it again, Delaney. Please. Tell me 'hello'."

He kissed her. He would have sat there and gone up in flames if he hadn't, but Hannah's soft, wet mouth did nothing to put out the fires raging all through him. Her ardent response only inflamed him more.

She didn't taste like peppermint Schnapps as she had when he'd kissed her before. Now she tasted like some kind of exotic, edible flower. Candied violets and wild orchids and the sweetest of sugarcoated blooms greeted his tongue when it touched hers.

He circled his arms around her, bringing her close against him, feeling again how warm and lush her flesh was under its cool, thin covering of satin and how delicate were the bones beneath that. Her heart, he could tell, was beating as hard as his.

Almost before he realized it, he had lowered her back onto the mattress and repositioned himself to allow his good left hand to slide beneath the folds of her gown and discover all the sleek temptations hidden there. Her soft sighs began to turn to husky moans as he touched her here, there, everywhere. He couldn't stop. Never in all his disreputable past had a woman come so sweetly alive at his fingertips. Never had he felt himself so dangerously close to the edge of his control. Especially when she whispered, "Oh, yes. Oh, please."

"Hannah." His voice was thick with desire. "Judas, how I want you. But..."

"Please."

Delaney raised up above her, just enough to see the passion in her eyes and her lips glistening from his kiss. He couldn't stop now, even if he wanted to. He knew that. Maybe Hannah couldn't either. But she had to know the truth.

"This isn't a proposal of marriage, darlin'. You need to know that." He searched her expression, looked deeply into her eyes. "It doesn't mean I'm staying. It is what it is, Hannah. I'll let you decide."

"Decide?" she echoed, hearing the breathlessness in her own voice, hardly believing it was her own. There was nothing to decide, she told herself, because from the first time she'd laid eyes on this man it seemed this coming together was their destiny. Even Ezra had seen that. Even Ezra had known. And he had given them his blessing, hadn't he?

She pressed her palms against his whiskery cheeks, loving that roughness, wanting to know every texture of him, every taste. His eyes glittered as they searched her face.

"Love me, Delaney. Whether you go or stay. Love me now."

His mouth captured hers almost before her words were spoken. Her breath became his. Every inch of her burned beneath his touch, then yearned for it again when his hand moved elsewhere.

When he entered her, for a second Hannah held her breath as harsh memories of Memphis came rushing back. Memories of rough hands, whiskied breath, big bodies that pressed her own starved frame into a stained straw mattress. Then, just as she felt her body stiffen, Delaney's deep voice sounded warm at her ear.

"It's all right, darlin'. I won't hurt you. Relax. Let me love you all slow and easy."

In response, she felt her muscles—every one—relax. Even her bones seemed to soften. All of her was melting suddenly, then just as suddenly going up in flames like hot tallow. Waves of flames like an ocean on fire. A burning tide ripped through her.

"Delaney...!" she cried at the same moment he groaned her name.

They lay quietly then, his warm body like a blanket over hers, their breathing slowing down in unison while Hannah's mind drifted into a peaceful place she'd never been before.

"Delaney," she sighed as she fell asleep within the circle of his arms.

It had been a good long time—maybe years—since Delaney had held a sleeping woman in his arms. He had forgotten the pleasure of it and the deep satisfaction of that intimacy.

He hadn't loved her slow and easy as he'd promised, but rather like a wild summer storm that blows up fast and carries off everything in its path. Only for a brief moment had she seemed reluctant, and he wondered if that wasn't because they were lying in Ezra's bed where she must have lain so many nights before.

He should have thought of that, he told himself, then admitted he hadn't thought of much of anything except making love to Hannah. And now he wished he hadn't. Dear God in heaven, what had just happened between them was going to make leaving her the hardest thing he'd ever have to do.

She stirred in his arms and gave a soft and sleepy

little laugh. "Close," she whispered. "See, we got close after all, Delaney."

"Gabriel," he said, curling his arms more tightly about her, burying his face in her hair.

"What?"

"It's Gabriel. My Christian name. You asked a while back."

"Hmm. Wasn't he one of God's angels?"

"I guess so," he answered.

Then later, after he was certain she had fallen back asleep, Delaney added almost wistfully, "But, Hannah, my sweet darlin', that's one thing I'm not."

Hannah woke, vaguely aware that she'd just heard the clock downstairs striking—what had it been?— four or five chimes. A moment later she realized she was back in her own bed. What had happened earlier seemed like just a lovely dream.

And yet it had been real. As real and as close as a man and a woman could be. Even as she smiled, she felt a slight puffiness to her lips. She stretched languidly, feeling the delicious ache of muscles she hadn't used in years, if ever.

Gabriel! Suddenly she remembered that Delaney had told her his name. God's angel. God's angel in the guise of a hard-muscled, gentle-handed man who had taken her to Heaven and beyond tonight.

Don't get used to this, Hannah, she cautioned herself. *Delaney was making love to you, not promises. He told you so.*

But still, she thought.

Oh, but still...

A warm tear spilled from the corner of her eye and dripped onto the pillowcase before she could swipe it or the ones that followed away. Then she whispered a soft prayer into the darkness of her room.

"Dear God, please let him stay. Please make Delaney stay. And Ezra, if you're up there listening... Oh, my dearest, I thank you with all my heart. No matter what happens, I thank you."

Chapter Sixteen

The next morning, after her lusciously long and warm bath, Hannah spent several anxious moments standing before the mirror in her room, peering into the glass, and wondering if last night showed somehow upon her face. Did her eyes sparkle just a bit too much? Was there a knowing lift to the edges of her mouth or a glow she hadn't worn before?

Having satisfied herself that there were no telltale signs of passion and that she merely looked rested and healthy, she trotted downstairs, only to stop abruptly on the landing when she heard Delaney's voice in the dining room. She had assumed he'd be gone by this hour. It was almost eight o'clock, for heaven's sake. Facing Florence and Abel and Henry was going to be difficult enough. But Delaney? She didn't think she could look at him without sighing or be near him without wanting desperately to touch him.

She'd just about made up her mind to retrace her

steps to the safety of her room when Abel called out, "Hannah? Is that you?"

Damn.

"Yes, Abel. I'll be right there." Composing herself, Hannah touched her hair, smoothed the black folds of her skirt, then gripped the bannister and forced her feet to carry her down and into the dining room.

Her heart did a giddy somersault when she saw the sheriff, who was just that moment returning his coffee cup to his saucer and missed it completely when she came into his view. The cup chattered against the rim of the dish before he got it properly settled. He met her eyes then, and his mouth—Lord, how she remembered its touch—slid into an odd, half-embarrassed little grin.

Hannah cleared her heart out of her throat. "Good morning, all," she said, trying not to sound too gay, too giddy, or too satisfied. "It looks like it's going to be a lovely day."

Abel rose and pulled her chair out. He resumed his seat then and said, "Mourning wear becomes you, Hannah. Most ladies don't look half so fetching in black. Funny I never noticed that before."

While she conjured up a response, she could feel the sheriff's amused eyes on her and imagine his secret grin, knowing why her color was high this morning, not to mention her spirits. Gracious! If she didn't tamp down on thoughts about last night, she'd be blushing and gushing like some silly schoolgirl.

"Thank you, Abel. I think there must be something in the air this fine summer morning." Hannah glanced down the table to her right. "You're looking well, Florence," she added brightly, hoping to divert everyone's attention elsewhere.

"I'd say she's looking quite beautiful," Henry Allen said immediately, leaning a little in Florence's direction, smiling like a young swain with one of Cupid's arrows stuck prominently in his breast.

"Why, Henry! How very sweet." Florence leaned away from him, however, and there wasn't the least hint of an arrow displayed on her tightly corseted bosom. Not one inscribed with Henry's name, anyway.

"Would you care to have supper with me this evening at the Sunflower Café, Florence?" he asked, lowering his voice only slightly, obviously unashamed of his newfound adoration.

"No, thank you, Henry," Florence replied. "It's very kind of you to ask, but I've made other plans."

The young banker paled and looked crestfallen for a second, then his face grew mottled with anger. He planted both fists on the table. "With him, I suppose. With that Dancer fellow. You don't know anything about him, Florence." He looked across the table then and fairly shouted, "Sheriff, do you?"

"Not much" was Delaney's terse reply, which didn't appear to satisfy young Henry one bit.

"Well, I can tell he's not a gentleman in any sense of the word, or the sort of person one should pin any hopes on,'' he said with a snort while glaring at Florence. ''Or,'' he added accusingly, ''entrust with one's spotless reputation.''

Oh, dear. Hannah sat up straighter. She had diverted far more attention than she'd meant to. ''Henry,'' she interrupted, ''I don't think this is the time or the place…''

''Thank you, Mrs. Dancer.'' Florence shot up from her chair. ''I quite agree. It isn't the time or the place. Nor is it anyone's business but my own.''

She slapped her napkin on the table and bustled out of the room and up the stairs, leaving a momentary and rather stunned silence in her wake.

Henry was the first to speak. He swore softly, then he, too, rose to leave, not in pursuit of Florence, but in the opposite direction, stalking toward the front door and slamming it behind him.

''My goodness,'' Abel murmured. He took a sip of his coffee. ''I'd say the course of true love seems to be running rather crooked of late.''

Hannah bit down on a grin, then glanced at Delaney only to find his expression neutral, giving no hint of their own somewhat crooked course, no inkling at all that their bodies had soared to heaven and back the night before.

Such heaven!

She wanted Abel to fold his napkin right this minute and then announce that it was well past time to leave for his office, allowing her to be alone with the sheriff again. She wanted to make everyone in New-

ton—in Kansas—in the whole wide world—disappear
so it would be just the two of them. She would have
made the daylight disappear just then, if that had been
possible, in order to be with him again, right then,
just the two of them, in heaven, in the dark.

But instead it was Delaney who rose and proclaimed it was well past time to get to work. When
he passed her chair, she imagined she could feel his
heat. Then, when he walked out the door, she felt cold
all of a sudden. A shiver ran down her spine.

"Are you all right, Hannah?" Abel softly inquired.

"Yes. Quite."

"He'll be back, you know." The old man's chin
pointed in the direction Delaney had gone.

She looked into his kind and sympathetic eyes.
"Oh, Abel. Tell me truly. Am I...are my feelings
really so very easy to read?"

He smiled and reached out to pat her hand. "Only
for those who love you, my dear."

"Those who love me." Hannah gave a tiny laugh,
wondering just who that list included, wishing with
all her heart that Gabriel Delaney's name were written
indelibly there.

Alec Dancer didn't usually show his face on Main
Street until late afternoon. When he did that day,
around four o'clock, Delaney was waiting at the
hitching rail outside the National Hotel.

The gambler gave him a greasy smile. "Morning,
Sheriff."

"Not quite," Delaney said. He'd been chewing on a toothpick while he waited for Ezra's son to emerge. Now he tossed it away. "I'd like to have a word with you, Dancer. Got a minute?"

"A minute," he answered. "I'm on my way to the livery stable to rent a horse and buggy, then I've promised to call for Miss Green at four-thirty."

"Going for a little ride with the schoolteacher, huh?"

"A picnic supper, actually. Why do you ask, Sheriff?" He pushed his low-crowned hat to a cocky angle. "You wouldn't be jealous, now, would you?"

The lawman didn't even dignify that with a response. "Miss Green's highly regarded in this town," he said. "But I guess you know that."

Dancer's affable smile disappeared, and his well-practiced, oily charm went with it. "What is it you're trying to say to me, Delaney? You're not the young lady's guardian. At least not as far as I'm aware."

"No, I'm not," he admitted. "But she's an inexperienced young lady, and I'd like to see her stay that way."

"Why? So you can have a little taste of cherry when you're through with my father's whore?" He turned his back on Delaney and began a brisk walk in the direction of the livery.

If he hadn't been on the working side of a badge right then, Delaney would have stalked after the gambler and plastered Alec Dancer's perfect nose all over his handsome face. If the law allowed imprisonment for insults, he'd have the son of a bitch by the short hairs and halfway to the jailhouse right this minute.

Delaney just watched him go, though, waiting for the gambler to make that one mistake that men like him never failed to make. It would happen, he knew, and soon enough. He only hoped nobody else got hurt when the inevitable came to pass.

That night it was well after one o'clock when he heard the buggy pull up out in front and then the not-so-steady tread of the schoolteacher's feet as she mounted the stairs.

Well, hell, he thought. She was a grown-up, despite her inexperience, and like all grown-ups, she was entitled to make her own mistakes. Dancer had been right about one thing. Delaney wasn't Florence Green's guardian. Only it bothered the hell out of him that the slick-combed dandy had chosen this particular female on whom to shower his attentions.

What was in it for him? he wondered. There was plenty of experienced and even eager female flesh available in town. As for mere companionship, there were single women far prettier and more personable than Florence. Hannah, for one.

The thought alone lured his gaze up to her portrait. He had left his pillow at the head of the bed tonight, needing to see her, just plain needing *her*. How many nights had Ezra lain here, he wondered, listening for her, waiting for her to come to him?

Or had it been the other way around? Maybe Ezra

crossed the distance through the dressing room to Hannah's bed. That, Delaney had already vowed, was something he wouldn't do. If Hannah wanted him, she knew where to find him. He wasn't going to initiate anything. It wasn't right, knowing he wasn't going to stay. It wasn't sane, chasing after something he couldn't keep.

But, God help him, if she came to him, Delaney knew he didn't have the will to turn her away.

And she did come, standing in the dressing room doorway for a moment, swaying like a pale ghost, whispering his name, and only crossing to the bed after he reached out a hand in silent invitation. He moved over to make room for her, lifting the sheet as she slipped beneath it.

It felt as if she melted against him then, her warmth flowing into him, her softness in perfect contrast to his hardness.

This time they didn't even speak, but greeted each other with a kiss that deepened instantly and hands that already possessed a knowledge of where to touch and how and when.

Then, when Hannah's whole body shuddered beneath his, he stifled her little gasp of pleasure with his mouth at the same time that he silenced his own deep, gut-wrenching moan. Then again, after they had lain quietly side by side a little while, the wanting came back, even more intense.

So it was the next night and the next. And each night after he had loved her to sleep, Delaney carried

Hannah back through the dressing room and tucked her into her own bed so that no one would be the wiser. And each day he tried his best to retain a neutral, even stoic, expression, to give no hint of the paradise that was his every night, to disguise the longing that was like raw hunger each day until she came through his door after midnight and fed him with her lush body until, at last, in the deep hours of the night, he hungered no more.

And then one night she didn't come.

He listened to the clock as it struck one, then two, then three harsh and almost mocking chimes. He reminded himself again and again of his vow not to initiate their passion. He cursed himself for ever giving in, and cursed her for apparently giving up when there was no future in their union.

In the adjacent room Hannah heard the clock strike three.

"Please." She whispered the word three times while she stared into the darkness overhead, waiting for Delaney to come to her.

An hour or so earlier, she had stopped still in the dressing room, her hand just shy of the doorknob that she'd turned each night before. Not tonight, she'd thought suddenly. Not tonight. I can't. I won't. Then, without making a sound, she retraced her footsteps back to her own bed.

It wasn't that she didn't want him. Dear Lord, she thought perhaps right now she wanted his strong body in hers even more than she had before. But she needed Delaney to come to her this time. It was suddenly crucial, although she couldn't have said why. Not pride, certainly. Hannah's pride had suffered no loss each time she crept into the sheriff's room. She had only felt welcome and warm and utterly fulfilled.

If anything, she decided, her need to have Delaney come to her—just once—had something to do with sharing this strange nighttime alliance of theirs. She needed to know it meant as much to him as it did to her. She had to know that he needed her—deeply and undeniably—as much as he wanted her.

It was important to her. Absolutely vital. And it was foolish, she thought now, like cutting off her nose to spite her face. He wasn't coming. He wasn't. And somewhere in her heart she realized she'd never be able to go to him again because her need for him far outweighed his mere physical desire for her.

She shouldn't have put him to the test. Dear God, she should have just gone on the way they were and never tried to strike a balance with their feelings. Need. Want. None of that mattered now.

If she continued to lie there staring up into the darkness, Hannah was certain that she would weep, so she lit the lamp beside the bed and scrunched her pillows behind her, ready to read until dawn if that was what it took to forget her deep disappointment. But no sooner had she opened her volume of tales by Washington Irving than the dressing room door creaked softly and slowly began to open.

Hannah stared, hardly breathing, and her heart held absolutely still. The door opened so slowly it seemed to take a century before she could see a hand on the inside knob, then an arm, and finally all of him. He'd put on his black trousers, in haste it appeared, for they weren't fastened and rode low on his narrow hips. His shirt hung open to reveal the fine sculpture of his chest.

Her lamp cast shadows on his somber face and glittered in his eyes, making the sheriff look dangerous for a moment. A wolf on the prowl. A wolf in winter, hungry and cold, seeking warmth and sustenance.

"I want you," he said, his eyes searching hers, searing into hers.

Hannah didn't answer. It was all she could do not to whisk off her covers and run into this arms, but she made herself stay, silent, on the bed, returning his intense gaze over the top rim of her book.

"Hannah," he said then, a rough but plaintive note in his voice.

She closed her book, but kept silent, watching the rise and fall of his chest, the nearly feverish look on his face while she tried to keep her own impassive, calm if not actually cool.

"Judas," he rasped. "Don't do this to me."

Wait, she commanded herself even as every nerve in her body was urging her to leap off the mattress and race into his arms. *Wait. Wait.*

"Hannah, please. I need you."

"Oh, yes." She sprang from the bed and rushed to

the bliss of his embrace and the hot, wild pleasure of his kisses.

Then he gathered her up in his arms and carried her to the bed. He hesitated before he put her down.

"Here?" he asked. "Are you sure? The memories, I mean. Of Ezra."

"There are no memories," she said. "Not of making love. Not here or in the other room. We didn't, Delaney. Ezra and I. We never once made love."

"But I...I thought..."

"We lived completely as man and wife?"

He nodded.

"No." Hannah sighed, tightening her arms around his neck, tilting her head against his shoulder. "I don't know why. Ezra couldn't. Or he wouldn't. Despite appearances, he was really a father to me. Never a lover."

He took in a long breath and let it slowly out. It was impossible to tell whether her revelation shocked or pleased him. She thought, though, that she felt his lips slide into a smile.

Then he lowered her onto the bed and reached for the lamp.

"No, don't," she said, touching his arm.

He looked at her quizzically.

Hannah smiled. "I want to see you when you're loving me, Delaney. Is that terribly shameless?"

His mouth hooked in the smallest of grins. "Yep." Then he shrugged out of his shirt and dropped it on the floor. "Shameless and brazen and just what I want, too."

She leaned forward, pressing a kiss on the soft vertical hairline of his abdomen. "I need you, too, Delaney. It's different from just wanting this."

"I know. Shh."

He tangled his fingers in her hair while his already unbuttoned trousers fell easily off his hips with just a nudge of Hannah's hands. Then, a moment later, he was working the tiny buttons at the throat of her gown.

And working them. His right hand had come up automatically to unbutton her high-necked nightdress, and Delaney found himself fumbling pitifully with the minuscule mother-of-pearl discs. What kind of man couldn't even summon up the skills to remove his lover's clothes? A little curse ripped through his teeth, just as Hannah's hand brushed his away and swiftly dispatched the buttons and then the gown itself.

At the sight of her beautiful lamplit breasts, after a taste of their rosy crests, Delaney forgot his disability. He loved her hard and gentle, long, thoroughly and well with what abilities remained.

"Hannah," he breathed against her ear as his sweat-soaked body relaxed into sleep. He couldn't imagine ever saying another woman's name that would feel so much like a prayer on his lips. He dreaded the thought of ever loving anyone else.

They slept late the next morning, twined naked in each other's arms, utterly and happily exhausted in

Hannah's narrow bed, only to be abruptly awakened by the clattering of tin cans and a fast buggy pulling up outside.

"We're married!" Florence Green cried out beneath the open window. "Yoo-hoo, everyone. We're married! Alec and I have tied the knot."

Chapter Seventeen

Hannah and the sheriff bolted upright in unison.

"What the hell..." Delaney muttered.

"Oh, my Lord," moaned Hannah. She was up and off the bed immediately, dashing around the room for clothes, slippers, her hairbrush. "That silly, stupid, harebrained woman. What in the name of almighty heaven has she gone and done?"

"Married her. I'll be damned." Delaney shook his head, scowling while his left hand did battle with the buttons up the front of his shirt.

"Here. Let me." Hannah put down her hairbrush and finished his last two buttons. She glanced up to see him gazing at her with a pained expression on his face. "It's all right, you know. They don't give prizes for buttoning, my dear."

He let out a soft curse.

Hannah took his nearly useless hand and lifted it to her lips, gently kissing each finger. "It doesn't matter. As long as it doesn't hurt." She pressed his open palm to her cheek and whispered, "Oh, it doesn't hurt you, does it? I couldn't stand that."

"It doesn't hurt. Hell, I wish it did," he said disgustedly. "At least there'd be some feeling there."

"There's plenty of feeling here." Her hand covered his heart just before sliding down past his undone belt buckle. "And here."

"Hannah," he warned in a voice already thick with desire.

"I wish we could just go back to bed, Delaney, right this minute, and let Florence and Alec and all the rest of the world go on without us," she said with a sigh. "It would. Just go on without us, I mean. Nobody would care. No one would even miss us."

But no sooner had those wistful words escaped her lips than there came an insistent rapping on her door and Miss Green's excited voice.

"Mrs. Dancer? Are you in there? Mrs. Dancer? We've just gotten married, Alec and I. Oh, do come down, please, and see us off."

Hannah blinked and stood there immobile. "See them off?" Florence was leaving town with Alec Dancer? Ezra's son was leaving behind this house?

"Brush your hair," Delaney ordered. He turned her toward the mirrored dressing table and gave her a gentle tap on her rump to set her off in its direction. "I'll meet you downstairs," he said as he exited through the dressing room door.

All hell—at least a goodly part of it—had broken loose downstairs by the time Hannah arrived. The vestibule was littered with hatboxes and suitcases, and Abel Fairfax was kneeling on one overstuffed piece of luggage, trying in vain to latch it.

He glanced up at Hannah. "They've married. Miss Green and Dancer. Have you heard?"

How could she not? Hannah felt like saying. "What about the house, Abel?" she asked. "What does this mean?"

"I'm afraid I haven't a clue, my dear," he said, then returned to the catches on the recalcitrant suit-case.

"Oh, Mrs. Dancer. There you are." Florence came bounding down the staircase with another hatbox in her arms. She dropped it and rushed to hug her land-lady. "Do be happy for me. At last all my dreams have come true."

"This is so sudden, Florence." Hannah took a step back and studied the schoolteacher's ecstatic face. "Are you quite sure you know what you're doing?"

"Oh, my, yes." She tugged Hannah to the front door and gestured to the buggy where Alec Dancer leaned ever so casually. "Isn't he elegant? Why, sometimes I can hardly breathe in his presence. And now he's my husband, Mrs. Dancer." Florence let out a startled little laugh. "Just think of it. I'm Mrs. Dancer, too."

Hannah smiled weakly as she peered at Ezra's son. His hat sat at a jaunty angle and so did the cheroot that was clamped between his teeth. The man looked less the happy groom than someone who'd just won a sweepstakes. What was he up to? Then she spied the sheriff coming from the side porch, shotgun at his side, and knew that Delaney was equally suspicious.

When the two men began to talk, Hannah strained to hear their conversation over the new bride's natterings. She couldn't. But after Florence dashed back upstairs for more of her belongings, Hannah picked up her skirts and strode to the buggy.

"I understand congratulations are in order," she said, offering her hand to the gambler.

"Why, Hannah," he responded with a leer and a touch of his lips to her hand, "I didn't know you cared."

She jerked her hand from his grasp. "Florence says you're leaving town."

"My bride is correct. We're leaving and we won't be back. That ought to please you no end."

"And the house?" she asked.

"It's yours. Or his." He gestured toward the sheriff who stood nearby. "I told you, I won't be back."

Now Delaney's deep voice joined them. "Turns out our Miss Green is an heiress, Hannah."

"What?" She whirled toward Delaney.

"Tell her," he ordered the gambler.

Alec Dancer laughed. "I can't believe nobody knew. Living here all this time. Little Florence Green from Pittsburgh, Pennsylvania, home of the Green Foundry and assorted other lucrative industries. Your schoolmarm is worth more than her rather pudgy weight in gold.''

Hannah could feel her jaw drop as much in surprise at the news as at Dancer's ugly tone. She couldn't think of a harsh enough reply to this monster. But as it turned out, there was no time for a reply because just then Henry Allen came running full tilt up the sidewalk, necktie flapping and his hat half off his head.

''I've just heard the news,'' he said, trying to catch his breath. ''It isn't true, is it? It can't be true.''

Florence appeared on the front porch then and waved to them all. ''Henry,'' she called. ''Have you heard the wonderful news? You've been such a dear. I wonder if you could help Mr. Fairfax with my bags.''

Looking crushed and utterly forlorn, the young banker climbed the porch stairs as if they were carpeted with fly paper and his shoes were fashioned from lead.

''Poor sap,'' Alec Dancer said as he lit a fresh cigar and leaned lazily against the buggy.

Hannah threw him a black look then charged up the front steps to have a word—several of them—with Florence. But how did one tell an ecstatic bride that her handsome groom had only married her for her money? How could she ever have the heart to dash this young woman's happiness on this, her wedding day?

She loitered on the porch rather than go inside

while Abel and Henry carried out bag after bag and placed them in the buggy. She chewed thoughtfully on her lower lip, then concluded it wasn't her business, after all. People didn't always marry for love. Hadn't she herself been ready to marry Delaney in order to retain her house? Ah, but that had been before she loved him.

The thought nearly buckled her knees. She loved him! Not merely wanted him or needed him. She loved him in a way she had never loved Ezra, loved him as much as life itself. If he left her, she thought desperately, then life would simply cease. What could possibly matter after that?

Then suddenly Florence was hugging her and crying tears of joy and promising to write. "And don't worry about what's left of this month's rent," she said. "I'm fairly well off, Mrs. Dancer. I don't think you ever knew."

"No, I never…"

Then Nancy was there with a fistful of daisies, jamming them in Florence's hand. "Here, Miz Green. I brung you these," she mumbled. "Best wishes and all that."

"You *brought* me a bouquet, Nancy. Not brung." Florence giggled then. "Oh, never mind. I'm not a schoolteacher anymore. I'm a blushing bride. Thank you, Nancy. Thank you ever so much."

Halfway down the porch steps, Florence turned back. "Well, goodbye everyone. Wish me luck."

"Florence," Henry called from the door. If he intended to say anything more, he didn't have the opportunity when the bride turned her back and fairly skipped toward the buggy.

It was Delaney who helped her up into the seat beside her groom while Alec Dancer cavalierly flipped his cigar away, resettled his hat on his head, and reached for the reins. He snapped the leather over the black mare's rump and the buggy shot forward.

Florence grabbed for her hat with one hand and used the other one to wave goodbye. Alec Dancer never looked back.

Poor Henry barely ate for the next two days. Even Nancy, who was usually oblivious of such things, took pity on him and baked a perfect, lattice-topped cherry pie which the young man only picked at.

"Poor Henry," Hannah said with a sigh as she lay curled in Delaney's arms. Now that Florence wasn't creeping up the stairs at midnight, she felt more comfortable going to his room not long after she had excused herself for the evening.

"He'll get over it," Delaney said. His voice had a tinge of coolness even though his hand was warm on her flank.

"Do you think Florence will be happy?" she asked.

He was quiet a minute, then said, "No. Probably not. People rarely are."

She nestled closer. "I'm happy."

His hand seemed to freeze in place then, and a

wave of fear rushed through her. Oh, God. She knew what he was going to say even before he said it.

"Hannah, I'm leaving. Tomorrow."

She knew that. He'd told her in no uncertain terms. But deep in her heart she hadn't believed he would. Especially now that they had been so close. She could feel a dark fissure beginning to tear inside her. A hole was opening in her heart, all its contents threatening to pour out.

"I love you, Gabriel Delaney." It was all she could manage to say.

He stroked her hip again, then his hand slid up to brush the tangles of hair back from her face. "I love you, too, Hannah. But that isn't going to make me change my mind and stay."

"Isn't love enough?" Her voice sounded tight as she choked back her tears.

"Enough? Honey, it's more than I've ever had in my whole life." He grasped her chin and made her look at him. "You're more than I've ever had in my whole life. If I could stay, Hannah, I would."

She pushed his hand away and turned her face to the wall. "Liar. You *can* stay, but you won't."

"All right. If that's the way you want to think of it."

"Then you might just as well leave now."

But when he levered up to do just that, Hannah wrapped her arms around his waist. "I didn't mean that. Stay. For as long as you can, even if it can't be forever."

He lay back down and gathered her in his arms, cradling her head against his shoulder. "A lawman doesn't know the meaning of forever," he said. "Just day to day, Hannah. Maybe not here in Newton. But in towns like Dodge and Tombstone."

"Tombstone." She shivered. "And that's where you'll go?"

"Yes. There's a job waiting for me. I sent a wire and got the reply this morning."

"You'll be the sheriff?"

"A deputy. My hand's—" He stopped abruptly.

"What?"

"Nothing."

"Your hand's what?" she asked. "Not fast or accurate enough for a hellish place like that? Is that what you were going to say?"

He nodded. "Something like that."

"Then stay here. Keep doing what you're doing. Keep doing what *we're* doing. I lived with Ezra fourteen years without the benefit of marriage, Delaney. I'd do the same with you."

"But I wouldn't," he said. "You deserve better than that, Hannah. Judas. Don't you understand? Find yourself a whole man after I'm gone."

"A whole man!" She shot up, her hands flailing for a minute then dropping helplessly into her lap. "What in blue blazes do you think you are, Delaney?"

"I know what I am. And it's not what I used to be, dammit, or ever will be again."

''Then be something different!''

When his only answer was a hard wall of silence, Hannah flopped back down, telling herself she had a choice right now of arguing with him during their last few hours together, trying in vain to convince him to stay, or accepting his decision and letting their last moments be full of warm and loving memories for them both.

Some choice, she thought bleakly. Still she edged closer to his solid warmth, touched him everywhere in hopes of memorizing all the rough and smooth of him, and invited him into her once more, pretending—only pretending—he would stay.

When she woke the next morning, he was gone— his body from her bed, his belongings from Ezra's room. Delaney wasn't the sort to belabor a goodbye, which was probably for the best. Hannah, if given the chance, quite easily could have dragged their parting out to thirty or forty years.

There was no one in the dining room so she walked out onto the front porch where she found Abel with the *Gazette* unopened on his lap, his hands lightly folded on top. Oddly enough, it was a beautiful day with sunshine and butterflies already playing in her rose bed, and a faint breeze riffling through the grass and the leaves.

''He's leaving today, Abel,'' she said, surprised that her voice sounded so calm and almost matter-of-fact.

"Yes, I know. It didn't work out the way Ezra planned." He sighed. "For a while there, I had hoped..." His voice drifted off into silence.

"So did I," she said.

"Stubborn, that Delaney. Hard as nails." The old man shook his head. "I guess we had him pegged all wrong. I'm sorry, Hannah."

"I'm sorry, too." Sorry he was leaving, she thought, but she didn't have a single regret that she had loved him as she had. She'd do it again if she had the chance.

After gazing down the street to see the empty chair in front of the jailhouse, Hannah squeezed her eyes closed and compressed her lips. If she started crying now, if she shed so much as a single tear, there would be no end to crying. It would feel like dying, and that was no way to live.

"Well, I'd best see to Nancy before the kitchen's all in ruins," she said, turning to the door. Once inside, she added over her shoulder, "Pork roast for supper, Abel. You won't want to be late."

"Hannah," he called to her.

"Yes?"

"Maybe we were a little bit hasty."

She stood in the vestibule, frowning. What on earth was he talking about? "Hasty about what?"

"Delaney," Abel called. "He's coming back."

Her heart shot into her throat at the same time Hannah shot back out the front door. He was coming back, all right, walking at a good clip with his shotgun cradled in one arm. He looked purposeful if not downright determined. And to Hannah he looked like God's angel on a mission of the highest importance.

Please, she prayed. Oh, please. She could see that he still wore his badge pinned to his black coat. He hadn't quit yet. Not the town. Maybe not her.

Delaney took the porch steps two at a time, leaned his gun against the railing, then pulled a folded paper from the breast pocket of his coat.

"This just came," he said, "from Dodge."

He glanced at Hannah's lovely and expectant face as he opened the telegram, and knew she thought he'd changed his mind. It made him feel sick for a minute, and rather than let her believe in miracles a second longer, he handed her the wire. While she read, he apprised Abel of its contents.

"They found Florence Green beaten nearly dead in an alley in Dodge. No identification on her, but she was able to say her name and address. That was all before she became unconscious."

"My God," Abel breathed.

"Require your assistance in locating next of kin," Hannah read out loud, then looking up at Delaney.

"I'll locate her next of kin," he said grimly, "and then I'm going to see that he gets twenty years in prison right before his eternity in hell."

"Alec Dancer did this?" Hannah asked.

"Who else?" Delaney answered.

"Who else, indeed." Abel hoisted himself out of

his chair. He slapped his newspaper across an open palm. "Good God, we should have seen this coming. We shouldn't have let her go."

"Hindsight's not worth much, Abel," Delaney growled, and then he looked at Hannah. "I need somebody to come with me to bring Florence back. There's a train in forty minutes."

He held his breath then, half expecting her to tell him it wasn't his job anymore and she'd just as soon see him riding a train to perdition. He was even ready to take a blow across his cheek when she stiffened her shoulders and solidly met his gaze.

"I'll pack," she said. "It won't take me more than a few minutes."

Chapter Eighteen

The train was more than hot. It was like riding in an upholstered oven, Hannah decided, and by the time they reached Dodge City at five o'clock that afternoon, she felt altogether cooked inside her black petticoats and widow's weeds.

They hadn't spoken much as they travelled the hundred and fifty miles. Delaney looked tired and his face more grim than she had ever seen it. Her own, she supposed, was the same. And though she had longed to spend more time with this man, this was not the way she wanted to do it. God only knew what awaited them once they reached their destination. Poor Florence could have perished, in which case Delaney would be hunting Alec Dancer for murder rather than assault.

She found herself crying softly into her hanky at one point, and the sheriff reached over and took her left hand with his right in a warm grasp that was reassuring and unsettling both. Hannah hardly dared to imagine his using a pistol or a shotgun with any accuracy when mere buttons brought him down. Frightened for them, she cried a little harder, for Florence and Delaney both. There were tears for herself, as well.

When the train pulled into Dodge, Delaney wrenched her valise from the brass rack overhead, picked up his shotgun, then insisted on carrying both objects, only to have Hannah's bag suddenly knocked out of his weakened grip by a young boy who was rushing pell-mell down the narrow aisle. Hannah promptly retrieved the bag and refused to give it back.

"It isn't heavy," she told him when he scowled, "and, besides, I'd rather you carried your gun."

If his mood had seemed gray before, it deepened to black after that incident, and stayed that way during their brief visit at the Dodge City sheriff's office. The sheriff was out of town, as it turned out, leaving one of his assistants in charge. The man's name was Tom Nixon, and he had jumped up, all smiles and chuckles, when Delaney walked through the door, then whacked him on the back like a long-lost best friend.

Hannah wandered around the office, so much larger than Newton's, while the two lawmen quietly discussed particulars. There was a picture display on one brick wall which, from a distance, she assumed to be a rogue's gallery of criminals. On closer inspection, however, it turned out to be photographs of the various lawmen who had served a time in Dodge.

Delaney was there, third from the left, in a grouping of serious, dark-dressed men. He looked different to Hannah, and it took her a moment to realize that difference was because he was wearing a pistol and a gun belt that angled rakishly across his hips. Despite the serious miens of the men in the photograph, Delaney seemed happier somehow than she'd ever seen him before. So, that was what he missed, she thought, suddenly acquiring a better understanding of what he meant when he said he could never be the way he used to be again.

"Florence is at the doctor's place across the street. Let's go."

Hannah jumped when she heard his voice so close behind her and felt his hand upon her back. She nodded her head toward the photo. "I was just…"

"Yes. I know." He didn't give it a glance. "Come on. Let's go."

He grasped her elbow with his good hand and guided her across Front Street, angling them between pushcarts and wagons and carefree cowboys afoot or on horseback who were obviously getting an early start to the evening. The doctor's office sat wedged between a hardware store and a saloon. Delaney knocked, and the door was opened by a woman in a stained gray apron.

"Yes?" she asked.

"We're looking for the young woman who was hurt yesterday, ma'am. Miss Florence Green. Or maybe she's going by the name of Dancer now. Tom Nixon told us she was here."

"Oh, of course. Please, come in." The woman stepped back to let them pass into a small waiting room ringed by mismatched wooden chairs. "I'm Elsa Bishop. I help my husband here."

"Is Florence all right?" Hannah asked.

"She was beaten very badly. As near as we could determine, there are several broken ribs, one fractured wrist, and a possible concussion. Once you see her, I think you'll see for yourselves what a brutal attack it was."

"I need to ask her a couple of questions," Delaney said. "Can we see her?"

"Yes. I can't guarantee she'll be able to answer any of them, however, the poor thing." Elsa Bishop sighed. "Follow me."

They did, along a narrow corridor and then to a small room lined with glass-fronted cupboards that were crammed with medical supplies. The curtains were closed, but even so Hannah could see poor Florence on the narrow cot against the back wall.

"Oh, Florence," she said, kneeling down beside the wooden cot and witnessing the damage that had been inflicted on the schoolteacher. One eye was swollen shut while the other was horribly bruised. Her lips were hardly recognizable as such, the lower one split and currently held together by several blood-stained threads.

"Florence," Hannah whispered, delicately touching her matted hair. "It's Mrs. Dancer, dear. It's Hannah. Delaney is with me. We've come to take you home.''

A tear dribbled from the young woman's swollen eye. She moaned softly, as if it hurt to utter even the smallest of sounds.

"Who did this to you, Miss Green?" Delaney asked.

Florence moaned again.

"It's difficult for her to speak," Elsa Bishop said from behind them. "The stitches, you see. And the injured ribs."

Delaney knelt down next to Hannah. "You don't have to talk, Miss Green. Just nod twice for yes. It was Dancer who did this to you, wasn't it?"

She gave two painful nods as more tears dripped from her eyes. Then, with obvious difficulty, she attempted to speak. "My dowry. Par...parents wired bank draft. Alec... Alec..."

"Stole it from you," Hannah finished.

Florence Green nodded, twice, then turned her beaten face to the wall.

The sheriff swore under his breath, then he stood and started for the door. Hannah struggled up. "I'll be right back," she told the doctor's wife, and rushed after him.

"Delaney, wait." She caught his arm just before he was opening the door to the street. "Where are you going?"

"Dancer's been on a two-day losing streak at the Lady Gay saloon. According to Tom Nixon, anyway.

That's why he hasn't been in any hurry to leave town.''

"What are you going to do?"

"I'm going to make him wish he'd left two days ago." His voice was as harsh as his expression. The color of his eyes had turned a fearful green like skies just before a violent storm.

She knew there was nothing she could say to dissuade him, and a part of her didn't even want to in the hope that he would make Alec Dancer pay dearly for what he had done.

"Be careful," she breathed, lifting on tiptoe to kiss his cheek.

"Stay with Florence. I'll be back."

She watched him stand outside on the planked sidewalk then, quite still except for the expansion and contraction of his black coat while he breathed deeply, while he slowly opened and closed his right hand. He stepped off the sidewalk into the street, disappearing behind a wagon full of barrels, while Hannah prayed she would see him again. Alive.

She continued to pray while she sat by poor Florence's bed, all the while listening for gunshots in the distance. Close by, though, voices rose in the hallway.

"You can't go in there," Elsa Bishop said.

"You can't stop me."

Even though she had never heard the voice raised in such anger, Hannah recognized instantly that it belonged to Henry Allen. She went to the door and opened it on his agitated face.

"Henry! What are you doing here?"

"Do you know this man?" Elsa Bishop asked.

"Yes. He's a friend of Miss Green's. It's all right, Mrs. Bishop."

The doctor's wife sighed. "Please don't stay too long. The poor woman needs her rest."

Once inside the room, Henry Allen rushed to the cot. He took Florence's hand.

"Oh, my dearest. What has he done to you?"

Florence cried out in pain, then, and Hannah touched Henry's shoulder.

"Her wrist is injured, Henry," she said quietly. "Just talk to her."

With infinite care, the young man placed Florence's hand beside her and released it. He bowed his head then, and his shoulders shook. "She isn't going to die, is she?"

"I'm sure she'll be fine," Hannah said. "It will just take time and tender care."

"I have time," he said. "Oh, and so much tender care to give."

"Then Florence is a lucky young woman, after all," she replied.

At first it had seemed quite normal for Henry to have appeared, but suddenly Hannah wondered how he had known about Florence in the first place. Certainly Delaney wouldn't have shown him the telegram. He'd been in too much of a hurry to leave town.

"How did you know, Henry? About this, I mean?"

"Jim Spangler at the telegraph office. He's a friend. I've confided my feelings about Florence to him." He turned his wet gaze up to Hannah. "I sat in the second class car on the train, then I followed you and the sheriff."

"You shouldn't have," she told him, quietly, without actually chiding him.

"I had to."

"She'll be fine, Henry. I'm sure. We'll take her home just as soon as Sheriff Delaney brings in Alec Dancer. He's over at the Lady Gay right now doing just that."

Henry stood up and wiped his eyes. "The Lady Gay? Where's that?"

"I'm not exactly sure."

"Never mind. I'll find it."

Henry's voice was different suddenly. No longer the worried would-be suitor, he sounded more like an enraged spouse. To Hannah's surprise and horror, he reached under his suit coat and brought forth an evil-looking, long-barrelled gun.

"There'll be no bringing in, Mrs. Dancer. No trial. No ten or twenty healthy years in jail." His placid lips drew back in such a vicious snarl that Hannah hardly knew him. "I mean to see that the bastard truly suffers for what he did. I hope to God I kill him."

"Henry, don't do this. Let Delaney—"

"Bring him in?" he shouted. "Over my dead body!"

Henry shoved the pistol back in his belt and charged for the door, brushing Hannah's hands aside. She couldn't stop him. She knew that. He wasn't a big man, but his fury had doubled his strength. The best she could do was run after him.

But before Hannah could jam her skirts through the door, Florence gave a muffled cry, wrenched her battered body to a sitting position, then—with a terrible thud—rolled onto the floor.

"Mrs. Bishop!" Hannah screamed as she turned back to help poor Florence.

Delaney stood at the long, opulent bar of the Lady Gay, his boot on the brass rail and his back to the crowd, watching in the mirror while Alec Dancer lost hand after hand after hand at a table across the smoky room. The gambler hadn't seen him come in. Delaney was certain of that. The man was focused intensely on the cards in his hand. Winners tended to banter and gaze around the room, but Dancer's eyes were for his cards only and his lips were tightly compressed.

He wondered just how much of Florence's fortune the man had lost. A lot, from the looks of it.

"So, you back for good, Delaney?" Harry Davis was wiping glasses on the working side of the bar, looking for conversation to make his twelve-hour, stand-up stint go a little faster. "The Earps are gone. I guess you knew that."

"Yeah, I knew." As soon as the words were out of his mouth, Delaney regretted them. Harry's mouth went a long way with a very little encouragement.

"Still in the law business?"

This time Delaney ignored the question, for all the good it did.

"Reason I ask is 'cause you're carrying that shotgun, there." He peered over the bar. "Haven't seen one of those in a while. Reminds me of Doc Holliday."

"Yeah." He tugged his hat brim lower, picked up his warm beer and turned, leaning his back against the bar, hoping like hell that Alec Dancer continued to be mesmerized by his losing pairs and busted flushes.

He hadn't quite decided how he'd take him. Considering his shotgun, The Lady Gay was dangerously crowded. And even though Dancer looked wrung out, Delaney wasn't sure he could take him down without a weapon. He and his ruined hand could probably use a little help, he thought bleakly, but he hadn't even bothered to ask Tom Nixon, who owned a piece of this saloon and got a cut from all the high-stakes games. Tom was the last person who'd want to see Alec Dancer led away from that lucrative table.

Just as he was deciding his own best bet was to go outside and reenter the saloon through the back door, behind Dancer's back, Delaney's gaze flicked to the bat wing doors in front. For a minute he didn't recognize the man with the glittering rage in his eyes and the long-barrelled pistol in his hand. Then he knew it was Henry Allen, bent on bloody revenge and about to get himself killed.

"Where's Alec Dancer?" Henry yelled over the noise of the crowd.

Delaney picked up his shotgun and moved toward the young banker. Nobody had paid much attention to his first shout, so he yelled again, louder.

"I'm looking for a son of a bitch who calls himself Alec Dancer."

By the time the room fell still, Delaney was only a foot or two away from Henry, trying to figure out how he'd get the banker's gun, keep hold of his own, and defend them both from the gambler, all without hurting half a dozen innocent bystanders.

What happened next unfolded in slow motion, the way such confrontations always did, whether one was on the receiving end of a bullet or not.

Chairs scraped and clattered over as the crowd sought cover—behind the bar, the piano, tables turned over as makeshift shields.

At the high-stakes poker game, the other players scattered when Alec Dancer stood up, cursed, and threw his cards on the green felt tabletop. Probably his first winning hand of the day, Delaney thought, oddly and inappropriately amused for a split second.

The banker's pistol came up just as the gambler's two-shot slid down his sleeve into his hand.

Now!

Delaney went for Henry Allen's gun just as the whole world seemed to explode in gunfire. He clutched the pistol in his left hand, took what he prayed was a solid bead on Dancer's heart, then fired at the same instant the gambler got off his second shot. The bullet ripped into his shoulder like a branding iron, blurring his vision for a second, distracting him just long enough for Henry Allen to try to wrest the shotgun from his right hand.

And then he saw it coming—death—hooded in black—astride a black horse. He'd already cocked both barrels, but the banker didn't know that. When Henry wrenched it away, the side-by-side exploded.

He heard glasses and bottles shattering behind the bar, then heard chunks of mirror raining on the floor. For an absurd second, Delaney wanted to laugh because he hadn't been hit.

Then his knees buckled and he saw the blood-stained sawdust floor coming up to meet him.

Chapter Nineteen

"Lady, if you're going to faint, you get out of here right now," Doctor Bishop warned Hannah. "I've got all I can deal with right here on this table."

"I'm fine. I promise. Please don't make me leave him."

"Then move away and quit blocking my goddamned light," he snapped.

Hannah didn't know how to move until Elsa Bishop took her by the shoulders and propelled her to a chair between two cupboards.

"Vern's a good doctor," Elsa said. "He'll take care of him. You'll see."

"Speaking of seeing, Mrs. Bishop," the doctor growled over his shoulder, "get back over here and give me some more goddamned light."

Elsa wiped her bloody hands on her apron, then scurried back to the table and raised a lantern high over the body lying there, his features pale and slack now after a dose of chloroform, and his blood-slick chest barely registering breath.

"Don't die," Hannah whispered to herself and to God. She had thought he was dead when she flew through the doors of the Lady Gay and saw Delaney face down on the floor and Henry Allen standing over him with a shotgun that still had smoke curling up from its barrels.

"I didn't mean to do it," Henry kept repeating. "I didn't mean to do it. He's dead. I've killed him."

"He's not. I won't let him be dead," Hannah had snapped, falling on her knees beside Delaney's body, trying to turn him over so she could see his face, could reassure herself that he was breathing. "Somebody help me," she cried.

Two men had squatted down and turned him over. With so much sawdust clinging to his clothes, Hannah hadn't been able to tell where he'd been shot. She brushed the debris from his hair and face. "Delaney," she whispered. "Oh, my love."

Then his eyes had flickered open, searching for hers, finding them for a second before falling closed again. He was alive!

"He's alive," she had screamed. "Oh, help him. Somebody help him please."

Now, sitting in one of Doctor Bishop's cramped surgery rooms, Hannah stared bleakly at some little bits of sawdust on the floor. They had probably left a trail from the Lady Gay to this little room, she thought. A terrible, bloody trail.

Dear God, don't let him die. I'll let him go if you'll only keep him alive. I'll give him up if you'll just give him back his life.

"Ma'am? Can I see you a minute?"

Hannah blinked and looked up into the face she recognized as Tom Nixon, the assistant sheriff.

"Outside," he said, taking her arm and ushering her out of the surgery room, along a corridor, and into the waiting room where he guided her to a chair.

"Ma'am," he said, "I know this isn't a good time, but the coroner needs some information on the fellow who was killed."

It was only then that Hannah was aware of the other man in the room. He tipped his bowler hat to her and withdrew a small notebook from his coat pocket, then proceeded to ask her too many questions.

Alec Dancer was dead, she kept thinking while she attempted to tell them everything she knew about him. Not much as it turned out. His name. His last address in Newton. Florence, his unfortunate next of kin.

The man was about to snap his notebook closed, then stopped. "Well, as long as I've got you here, I might as well collect some particulars on the other one."

"What other one?" she asked.

"Why, Delaney, ma'am. I heard he's not going to make it." The coroner turned to the sheriff. "Too bad. He was a good man and an even better lawman when he was here. Right, Tom?"

The lawman nodded.

Then, as Hannah stared in horror, the coroner made a little notation in his book, paused, and said, "That's funny. I can't for the life of me recall Delaney's Christian name. You don't happen to know it do you, ma'am?"

"Yes," Hannah said. She stood up, hands clenched at her sides, tears stinging her eyes. "But you're not going to need it for that damnable book of yours, sir. Excuse me, please. I have to...I must get back."

It was the longest night of her life. Every time Hannah heard another metal clink of buckshot in Dr. Bishop's enamel pan, she winced. The surgery took hours—clink!—clink!—until her face felt frozen in pain.

Finally, at four in the morning, the exhausted doctor put down his delicate pliers and said, "Well, I think I've got them all. Put the dressing on, Elsa, and then we'll let the good Lord do His work."

After everyone was gone, and while God held His angel in His hands, Hannah did, too. His left hand was cold, oh so cold, but she kept it warm between her own. Once or twice, her head jerked up when sleep tried to make her abandon her watch.

Then just after daybreak, when sunshine started filtering into the bleak little room, Delaney squeezed her hand. The pressure was faint, but real all the same.

"Hannah?"

"Yes, love?" She leaned close, let her lips brush his. They were parched, but warm. Warm with life.

The ghost of a smile passed across his mouth before it tightened again. "Don't let..."

"What? Oh, dearest, I can't hear you."

He drew in a breath that made him groan. "Don't...don't let them take my arm, Hannah. I'd rather be dead."

"Shh. They won't. You're going to be fine now. It's all over."

"Promise me."

"Shh. The doctor..."

He squeezed her hand then with surprising force, crushing her fingers together. His eyes glittered fiercely. "Promise me. Swear it."

"Yes," she whispered. "I promise. I promise with all my heart."

"Good. Good." His breath riffled out then, his wild eyes losing focus and his grip going slack as he drifted back into unconsciousness.

In less than twenty-four hours, Hannah was forced to keep her promise with a vengeance.

She had refused to take a room at the hotel, as encouraged to do by the Bishops. Elsa seemed to understand her need to stay beside the man she loved, but the doctor didn't take kindly to a woman refusing to do what she was told. Especially by him.

"You stay out of my way then, missy," he told her. "It's bad enough to be tripping over boxes of bandages and pills everywhere I turn without having one more stubborn female underfoot.''

When she wasn't incurring Dr. Bishop's wrath, Hannah bore the brunt of Henry Allen's misery.

''It's all my fault,'' he kept insisting. ''All of it.'' He had taken Florence to a nearby hotel once her condition had improved a bit, but he kept wandering back to the doctor's place, wringing his hands and wailing and wanting to be consoled if not forgiven.

Half the time Hannah wanted to throttle him and tell him that, yes, it was all his fault and she wished it were him lying in that little room instead of her Delaney. It didn't seem to matter to the banker that the local law hadn't found him at fault. The official word, she heard from Elsa, was that Delaney had shot Alec Dancer in self-defense and the shotgun blast was accidental.

''There won't be any inquiry,'' Elsa had said. ''Delaney's got a solid reputation here in Dodge City. You can take some comfort in that.''

But Hannah's only comfort was in watching Delaney breathe. And then, near dawn on the second day, that breathing became labored and harsh when the infection set in.

''I was afraid of that,'' Dr. Bishop said. ''Elsa, let's get ready. Bring plenty of rags along with my saw. The new one that came in from Chicago last week.''

''No,'' Hannah said, surprised by the calmness of her own voice and the steadiness of her hands as she raised Delaney's shotgun and pointed it at the doctor.

She didn't know whether or not the gun was loaded, but then neither did Bishop or his wife.

"I promised him," Hannah said.

"Don't be foolish." The doctor clucked his tongue. "He'll die if we don't…"

"I promised him," she said again. "Do everything you can, but don't do that."

"Then there's nothing I can do," he said flatly.

"All right. Then go." She kept the gun aimed at his midsection, her finger curled around the trigger, her gaze unfaltering.

"You're making a terrible mistake, missy."

"I'm keeping a promise," Hannah replied.

But when the doctor was gone, slamming the door in his wake, Hannah wasn't so sure of herself anymore. Her hands began to tremble as she placed the shotgun on the floor, and shook even more violently when she soaked a washcloth and smoothed it across Delaney's feverish face.

"Don't you die on me, Delaney. Do you hear me?" Hot tears streamed from her eyes and mixed with the water meant to cool him. "I kept my promise. You owe me now. You owe me."

She talked then. For hours she kept talking, yammering on, making sense or babbling nonsense while she bathed his burning skin, as if he wouldn't, couldn't die while she conversed, as if her words alone provided a kind of magic shield that was keeping death at bay. She crooned to him, coaxed him, even cursed him back to life when she felt him slipping away.

By eight o'clock that evening, when his fever finally broke, Hannah cried out hoarsely for Elsa.

"He's better," the doctor's wife exclaimed, one hand on Delaney's forehead, the other on his wrist. "His pulse is strong. Out of the woods, I think."

"Thank God," Hannah croaked.

"But you? What happened to your voice?"

"I used it up," she said, smiling brightly just before she collapsed in a heap.

They must've looked like the walking wounded, Hannah thought, as she staggered down the steps of the train. She'd sent a wire to Abel and was happy to see him there, standing beside the surrey he had brought in which to take them the short distance home.

All of them. Florence with her bruised face and her splinted wrist and bound ribs. Henry, still beside himself with guilt. Delaney, his arm in a sling and still much too weak to protest where he was taken and much too sick to care. And Hannah, her voice almost back to normal now, who was happier to be home than she ever thought possible.

She was even happy to see Nancy.

"We heard all about it," the girl said. She angled her head toward Delaney as Abel and Henry both helped him out of the surrey. "He all right? The sheriff?"

"Yes, thank God. He's all right, Nancy. Is Mr. Ezra's bed made up?"

"Yep. He's staying then? For good?"

The question startled Hannah. She'd spent so much time praying for Delaney's life that she hadn't bothered to think about where that life would be spent.

"He's staying for now," she answered, for that was all she really knew.

Behind her, at the surrey, voices rose. Hannah hurried over just as Abel was saying, "Well, walk on into town then, you damned fool."

"What in the world is going on?" she asked.

"Some people," Abel said, jerking his head toward the sheriff, "would just as soon fall down as lie down, I guess."

"It's the middle of the damned day, Abel. Some people have work to do." Delaney reached into the surrey for his shotgun, grimacing with pain, cursing through clenched teeth.

"Hannah, maybe he'll listen to you." The old man threw up his hands and stalked off.

"I doubt it," she muttered, crossing her arms and standing there, glaring at the man who'd been so close to death only days before.

He glared back. "Don't say a word, Hannah. I'm not in the mood."

"I wasn't planning to. I'm going to stand right here, nice and quiet, and watch you take a couple of steps then fall flat on your face. Maybe I'll call for help. Or maybe I'll just leave you lying in the yard. I haven't decided yet.''

He stood there still glaring, his breath starting to come hard.

"Go on," she said, pointing a finger toward town. "The day's a-wasting, Sheriff."

Now, while she watched, what little color he had in his face disappeared. "Judas," he murmured, widening his stance, wobbling.

"A little dizzy, are we?" Hannah took the shotgun from his hand and laid it back in the surrey. "There. Now you won't shoot yourself when you go over like a tree."

He swore again, his mouth curling half in pain and half in amusement. "You're a hard woman, Hannah Dancer."

She laughed. "I'm a strong one, too. Here." Hannah bent down and came up beneath his left arm. "See."

"All right," he said with a sigh. "I guess I won't be heading for hell in a handbasket if I take a little lie-down."

"I guess you won't," she agreed.

Delaney's voice changed then. It got a little lower, a tad softer. "Lie down with me, Hannah, will you?"

"Why, darlin', I thought you'd never ask."

For the next few days the Dancer place seemed more like a three-ring circus than a boardinghouse while Delaney and Florence recuperated. Henry took a leave of absence from the bank to stay by Florence's side. Abel would spend an hour or so at his office, then return looking to be helpful, but more often than not just getting in the way.

Doc Soames, for want of any other patients, called on them two times a day, then planted himself in the kitchen consuming cup after cup of coffee while Nancy tried to work around him. The mayor and the town councilmen visited Delaney twice, much to the sheriff's displeasure.

And then things quieted down dramatically when Florence and Henry departed for the East. Her parents had sent her money and demanded that she come home immediately, so Henry resigned his job at the bank to accompany her there. Hannah and Abel waved to them from the platform at the depot, and watched the former schoolteacher cling affectionately to the former banker's arm as they waved goodbye to her.

"I expect we'll be getting a wedding invitation soon," Hannah said a little wistfully. "I hope they can leave all the bitter memories of Dodge City behind them."

"They will," Abel replied. "Why, I can already see them spinning their grandchildren wonderful tales of the time they spent in the wild West."

Hannah laughed. "Wild, indeed. The house is going to be awfully quiet. Especially when…"

She hadn't meant to speak a word about the prospect of Delaney's leaving once he was well. She'd meant to keep that awful dread buried deeply in her heart. Having blurted it out now, Hannah felt tears welling in her eyes and threatening to spill down her cheeks.

"Maybe he'll stay," Abel told her. "You never know. That arm of his hardly qualifies him as a law-man anymore. At least not any place more lively than here."

"Maybe," she agreed, all the while knowing that if Delaney had felt less than whole two weeks ago, he was now feeling even worse. He still had his arm, but rather than being grateful for it, it seemed to serve only as a constant reminder of his disability.

"I'm worried about him, Abel. He should be healing faster. At times I fear he just plain doesn't want to get well."

"He was shot up pretty bad, Hannah. These things take time. He'll be fine. You'll see."

"I hope so."

But Hannah hardly knew what she hoped for anymore. When Delaney recovered, he would leave. If he didn't recover, if he continued to dwell in the dark, unhappy places of his soul, he would leave her in an altogether different way.

She slipped into his bed that night, as she always did, carefully so as not to wake him if he were asleep.

"It's quiet around here," he said.

Hannah smiled, curving her body close to his left side. "Yes. I never realized just how much noise Henry and Florence made. I hope they'll find great happiness."

"Finding it isn't all that difficult, Hannah," he

said. "You ought to be hoping they keep it. That's the hard part."

How well she knew, she thought as she reached up to touch his face.

"My God, you're burning up," she exclaimed, placing her palm flat against his forehead. "Delaney, why didn't you say something?"

"Why?"

"Why!" Hannah got up and lit the lamp. "You're hot as a stove and you're asking why," she muttered, shaking out the match then turning toward him. It frightened her to see his pallor and the glassiness of his eyes.

"You're in pain, aren't you? Don't lie to me, Delaney. I can tell."

"Honey, I've been in pain for a week now." A grin—a weak one—flared across his lips. "I'm pretty used to it by now."

"But this is worse," she said. "Isn't it?"

He didn't answer, but closed his eyes and tightened his lips.

"Isn't it?" she demanded. "Tell me, dammit."

"Yes," he said finally, turning his head away from her. "It's worse."

Just as the sun was coming up the next morning, Doctor Soames came down the stairs where Hannah sat on the bottom step. He had banished her from the bedroom an hour earlier when she had had to rush to the washbasin not once, but twice, to throw up.

"How is he?" she asked when the doctor lowered himself onto the step beside her.

"Sleeping. I gave him a pretty good dose of chloroform to keep him out while I was digging in his shoulder. He's liable to sleep all day."

"That's good," she sighed. "I might do the same myself. Will he be all right now, Doc?"

"Far as I can tell. I don't know who that butcher was in Dodge, but he left enough lead in Delaney to supply a small army. I even found an old slug from some past casualty that must've been giving him fits all this while. Got that all cleaned out, too. Hell, I'll bet he lost three pounds once I collected all that metal."

Hannah smiled. "That's good. I hope... Oh, Lord, Doc. I think I'm going to be sick again."

He grabbed the back of her neck and pushed her head down. "Take in some deep breaths. Deeper," he ordered.

"There," she said when he let her up. "I'm better. That's odd, Doc. You know me. I never get sick like that."

"You had your monthly of late, Hannah?"

"My..." Her eyes widened and locked on his. "Well, I..."

"I'm not saying that's what it is, mind you. Could be, though." He closed one eye in a wink, then whispered, "Could be you and that fella upstairs in Ezra's bed have some serious talking to do."

Chapter Twenty

"You sick again, Miz Dancer?"

Nancy's voice had all the warmth of a pickled cucumber just out of the jar.

"I'd go see Doc Soames, if I were you," the girl droned on, pinning damp linens on the clothesline, while Hannah straightened up and dabbed at her lips with a hanky.

"Thank you, Nancy. I just might do that." She tucked the hanky in her sleeve, whipped her skirts around and headed back to the kitchen door from which she'd exited in a hurry only moments before.

See Doc Soames, indeed. She'd seen the man last week after missing her second monthly, and after he'd poked and prodded her a bit, he'd confirmed that, yes indeedy, she was going to have a baby.

"You had that serious talk with the sheriff yet?" he'd asked her.

"No. Not yet. But I will."

"But you haven't yet, have you?" Hannah muttered to herself as she banged through the back door into the kitchen.

"Haven't what?" Delaney was standing at the stove, pouring himself a cup of coffee, looking even stronger than he had the day before, if that was possible. Once all the buckshot and bullet fragments were out of him, he had healed with amazing speed.

Hannah searched her brain for some answer to satisfy his curiosity, but just as she started to speak her gaze latched on the gun belt at Delaney's hips. He turned, coffee cup secure in his right hand, and that was when she saw the holster and the gun. For a moment she could hardly breathe.

"What's wrong?" He searched her face, his eyes full of worry. "Hannah?"

"Nothing," she said, then stuttered, "The...the gun."

"Oh." His mouth quirked in a sheepish grin. "I'm just trying it out." He lifted the coffee cup in a kind of salute, obviously pleased with the progress he had made and the newfound strength and agility of his hand.

"I'm happy for you," she said, trying to match her expression to her words.

Delaney set the cup down on the table, took two long steps, and gathered Hannah in his arms. Her resistance was brief—only a quick "Not here. Nancy will see"—before she melted into him. His right hand slid easily from her back to her breast and he gloried in the feel of her, the weight and warmth that his hand could now completely savor.

He was tempted to take her by the hand and lead her back upstairs to bed, to test a few other abilities that his hand had reacquired in the past ten days after the doctor had removed an overlooked piece of lead that somehow had been the cause of his bad hand.

Hannah had been sleeping in his bed ever since their return from Dodge, but they hadn't made love, not even after his nearly miraculous cure.

"Wait till you're all well," she would insist, and more insistently each night.

Just how well did a man have to get? he wondered now, breathing in the sweet fragrance of her hair. He tipped her chin up, lost himself in her eyes a minute, but then when he tried to kiss her, Hannah turned her face away.

"What's wrong, darlin'?" he asked.

Before she had a chance to answer, Nancy appeared, jamming her big wash basket through the back door and muttering about clothespins and horse flies and sick people who didn't have sense enough to see the doctor. Hannah jerked out of his arms and stepped away.

"Who's sick?" he asked.

"She is." Nancy jabbed her chin at Hannah. "And she don't care who catches it, either. I wouldn't stand all that close if I was you, Sheriff."

"Hannah?"

"Nonsense," she replied sharply. But then her face seemed to crumple. "Oh, dear," she whimpered, rushing out the door.

"Go away."

Hannah was sitting in a heap of black satin at the back of the yard. Delaney's long shadow cut across her skirts.

"Just leave me alone," she wailed.

"I'm taking you back to bed," he said, "and then I'm going to get Doc Soames. Whatever this is, Hannah, you can't ignore it. Hell, it's probably nothing."

"It's something," she said bleakly, dabbing her hanky to her lips.

"Then let the doc take a look at you."

"He already did."

"And?"

Hannah sighed. "You better sit down, Delaney." Or else you'll fall down, she was tempted to add.

He squatted beside her, his arms braced on his thighs, his expression so troubled that Hannah almost laughed.

"I'm not sick. At least not that way. Oh, Lord. I guess there's no getting around it. Sooner or later everyone's going to know."

She was babbling now and waving her hanky and beating around the bush, not knowing how to say the words that would certainly change their lives. Words that would bind him to her in a way she wasn't sure she could accept. Now, if he stayed, it wouldn't be of his free will.

"Hannah. Judas. Just tell me."

"I'm going to have a baby."

Even though he was already squatting down, his legs seemed to go out from under him.

"Mine." It wasn't a question.

"Yours," she said. "Ours."

"Hell of a surprise, Hannah."

She made a little murmuring sound, unable to think of anything else to say. Delaney was an honorable man. He would stay. She was miserable. It wasn't supposed to be this way.

He wasn't supposed to laugh, either, which was what he was doing now. Laughing like a damn fool.

"Stop it." Without thinking, she curled her hand into a fist and drove it into his shoulder. The blow not only caused him to quit laughing, but sent a swift curse whistling through his teeth. "I'm sorry. Your poor arm. I didn't mean…"

"It's all right. I wasn't laughing at you, honey. I was…" He reached in his coat pocket, produced a folded paper, and handed it to her. "Here. Read it."

She held the telegram as if it were a poisonous snake. "What is this?"

"Open it. Go on. Read it."

Hannah glared at the paper, turning it this way and that. "I don't like surprises, Delaney."

"Now that's a hell of thing to say after what you just sprung on me." There was no anger in his voice. There was amusement, threading through his voice and glittering in his eyes.

"Dammit, Hannah. Read it." He snatched the telegram, unfolded it, and put it back in her hands.

They were trembling now and the words on the paper jerked and jumped under her eyes.

"It's from Tombstone, Arizona," she said.

"Uh-huh. Go on."

Her gaze wandered down to the bottom. "It's signed Wyatt Earp."

"Is that a fact? Any more?"

She squinted. "It's dated yesterday."

"Yesterday, huh? And just what does ol' Wyatt have to say?"

Hannah had to brace her elbows on her knees to hold the paper still. "He says 'Many congratulations on your impending marriage. Sorry you won't be able to join us.'"

"Hmm."

"I don't understand," she said. Her head was reeling all of a sudden and the letters on the telegram were beginning to blur. She couldn't tell if she was about to laugh or cry. "What does this mean?"

Delaney took her face in both hands. "It means, Hannah, that I sent word to Arizona a week ago, saying I'd be staying on here. I've just had a little trouble formulating my speech."

"Speech?"

"My proposal of marriage, darlin'. I wanted to do it right." He grinned. "This is it, I guess."

"It," she echoed stupidly.

"My proposal."

"But...but your gun," she said. "When I saw you wearing it this morning, I was so sure you'd decided to leave."

"I'm still the sheriff, honey. I've got to make a living for us." He laughed. "Especially now that we've got one less room to rent out."

She stared at the telegram again, at yesterday's date in the corner. He had chosen freely. He had chosen her. If she hadn't already been sitting, Hannah would have hit the ground hard. As it was, she had to lean against Delaney's shoulder.

"You feeling ill again?" he asked, worry coloring his tone.

"No, not ill. I'm feeling wonderful. Happy. Amazed. However did this happen?"

"Ezra," he said softly.

"Ezra." Hannah sighed. "What a precious gift he gave us." She circled her arms around his waist and whispered, "Would you think it terrible of me if I wore black on our wedding day? In Ezra's honor? I won't, not if you disapprove."

Delaney shook his head. "Only if you promise me something."

"Anything. What?"

He drew her closer against him. "That after our wedding day, you'll never wear black again."

"I promise. But I won't have to, you know." She took his right hand and moved it to cover the child growing inside her. "Gabriel Delaney, I'm going to see that you live on forever."

"That'll be good, Hannah." His voice, already wistful, broke in his throat. "That'll be...whole."

* * * * *

If you enjoyed

THE MARRIAGE KNOT,

*turn the page for a preview of
Mary McBride's next Harlequin Historical,*

BANDERA'S BRIDE...

Prologue

Texas, 1866

It wasn't a perfect partnership, the one between the Southerner, Price McDaniel, and the half-breed, John Bandera. It was as far from perfect as the rugged landscape of south Texas was from the gentle hills of Russell County, Mississippi. The two men had almost nothing in common.

Physically, they were as mismatched as daylight and dark. McDaniel was a slight man with hair as fair as corn silk. John Bandera, the dark half of the equation, had bronze skin and cast-iron black hair. Part Comanche, part Mexican, and part anybody's guess, he was imposing in size alone, but it was his amber, catlike gaze that kept most men at a wary distance. His partner, Price McDaniel, was usually too drunk to be cautious.

When drunk, which was often, Price was a man

given to lengthy proclamations uttered in a drawl that was one third Mississippi and the rest pure Tennesse whiskey. John Bandera rarely drank and said little in return.

The two men didn't even particularly like each other. Still, they were partners, bound by a single and uncharacteristic burst of heroism at the Cimarron Crossing in 1864 when Lieutenant McDaniel had saved Scout Bandera's life.

Despite their differences, the partnership—thus far—had proven beneficial for both of them. The year before, after being mustered out of the army, Price had had more money than good sense, and he had wanted to build a ranch in Texas to rival anything back in Russell County, Mississippi. No matter that he didn't know a longhorn from a mule deer or a heifer from a steer.

John had been broke, physically as well as financially. The army had no use for a scout on crutches, and John had needed a place to heal. He'd owed Price for saving his life, and he figured one year of his sweat and expertise would cancel his debt to the Southerner.

Now that year was up.

The house was finally finished. Its pine floors and door frames glowed a rich gold beneath a first coating of shellac. The place still smelled of sawdust, but that raw odor mingled now with the fragrance of oiled walnut and rich leather.

Price McDaniel's furniture—two wagon loads all

the way from Mississippi—had arrived earlier in the day. There were wardrobes, chairs and sofas, dressers, mirrors, all manner of beds and bedding. There was one big swivel chair that matched one enormous desk. And there had also been one cream-colored letter tucked neatly inside the center drawer.

Price had been on a tear ever since finding it. He had read the letter at least a dozen times, and had looked at the enclosed *carte de visite* long enough and hard enough to wear the chemicals right off the little photograph. At the moment, the picture lay face down on the desktop, the envelope was strewn in little pieces on the flor, and Price was fashioning the letter itself into a rough approximation of a bird.

''Ladies,'' he slurred as he folded one edge of the vellum, then crimped it, ''especially those of the southern persuasion, are like gardenias. Have you ever seen a gardenia, John?''

As lamplight glanced off the fresh pine panelling, it made the half-breed's eyes all the more amber when he looked up from the list of supplies he was composing—goods intended to see his soon-to-be ex-partner through the coming winter.

''Nope,'' he replied, about to add that he'd never seen a lady, either. Instead he returned his attention to his list, knowing Price would go on with his drunken declamation whether anyone was listening or not.

He did, interspersing his words with laborious sighs.

"They're all pale and creamy and petal-soft. Dewy and cool to the touch. Only you can't. Touch them, I mean. Southern ladies are just for the looking. Touch them, and they bruise. Just like a gardenia. You remember that, John, if you ever have the supreme misfortune to meet up with one of them."

"I'll keep that in mind." His chances of meeting up with a lady, Southern or otherwise, were slim, slimmer, and none, John thought. The notion that he'd ever have the opportunity to touch one struck him as ludicrous. He'd learned early and at the painful end of a knife not to want what he couldn't have. Ladies were high on that particular list.

He made a last notation now on his own list, then parked the pencil stub behind his ear. "If you're all done ranting, Price, maybe we could go over a few things."

The Mississippian smiled sloppily as he lifted the folded letter, held it shoulder-high a second, then launched it across the room. The pale paper flew like a snub-nosed, stubby-winged owl before it plummeted to the floor beside John's moccasined foot.

John ignored it a moment, then picked it up and smoothed it out across his knee, instantly intrigued by the daintiness of the penmanship, trying to imagine the pale, fine-boned fingers that had drafted each delicate word.

He read not the whole, but separate, beautifully crafted words and phrases here and there. *How delighted we all were. Sympathetic to your dire circum-*

stances as a prisoner of war. Russell County. Do remember. Forever your home.

His amber eyes flicked up to meet his partner's. "You going back?"

Price chuckled softly as he filled his empty glass from the bottle near his elbow, then raised the glass in a wavering salute.

"Here's to Russell County, Mississippi, where a Russell is always a Russell and everybody else is…everybody else."

He downed half the whiskey, then continued. "And here's to Miss Emily Russell. May she bloom and prosper in Russell County soil. Here's to gardenias in all their pale and untouchable glory."

Price drained his glass and thumped it down on the desk top. "Here's to us, partner. And to the frigid day in hell that finds me back in Mississippi."

"You're staying." It wasn't a question so much as an acknowledgement. A disappointed one. John had hoped for a moment that Price would go home. It was where the man belonged, after all. So what if he had turned his back on the Confederacy in order to get out of a Yankee prison? He hadn't been the only Rebel prisoner who'd put on a blue uniform and headed west as a Galvanized Yankee.

But he didn't belong out West anymore. He belonged back home with well-bred gentlemen like himself and with ladies like gardenias. And he was damned lucky, in John's estimation, to have a place where he belonged.

"I'm staying." Price's clenched fists banged hard on the desk top. "Russell County be damned, along with all the Russells in it." He picked up the little *carte de visite* and, without even glancing at it, flicked it across the desk toward John. "Good riddance to them all."

John's dark hand shot out to catch the photograph before it fluttered to the floor. It felt warm in his palm, almost alive. He stared at its blank side a moment, as if hesitant to look at the face of the woman...no, the lady...whose delicate hand had composed the letter still lying on his leg. What face could be flawless enough? What pose perfect enough? What tilt of chin or hint of smile could be worthy of the lady in his head?

This one! His heart bunched up in his throat when he gazed at Emily Russell, and as his sun-bronzed thumb smoothed over the photograph, he wouldn't have been at all surprised to see her lovely image begin to wither and fade. What was it Price had said? *Touch them, and they bruise.*

John had to clear his throat before he spoke, but there was still an unfamiliar, nearly ragged catch.

"She's a lady, Price. You ought to write her back."

"Like hell," his partner snorted, replenishing his glass, sloshing whiskey over the rim. "Since when are you so concerned with proprieties?"

Since a minute ago, John wanted to say, but he merely shook his head and muttered, "It's the right thing to do."

Price rolled his eyes. "Well, you go on and write her, then, if you feel so strongly about it. Go on, John. Be my guest. Write the lady back."

He did. Then, although he'd meant to leave when that first year was up, John Bandera hung around waiting for a reply.

When it came—addressed to Price—he wrote her back.

And waited again. And again.

Six years later, long after his drunken partner had picked up and disappeared, John Bandera was still there, still writing letters signed "Price," still loving the lady so like a gardenia.

Chapter One

Mississippi, 1872

"Emily Russell, you are not leaving. I forbid it. Now, you put that suitcase down. Do you hear me? Put it down."

"I do hear you, Dodie. You're screeching like an owl, and I wouldn't be a bit surprised if everybody in Russell County hears you."

"You wouldn't be doing this if your brother were here. After all Elliot's done for you, too. How can you be such an ungrateful wretch?"

Emily shoved past her wailing sister-in-law, charged through the front door, and dropped her final piece of luggage on the veranda.

"There." She shaded her eyes against the bright morning sun, searching past the long sweep of driveway toward the street beyond. "Now, where in blazes is Haley Gates? He promised me he'd be here by ten o'clock."

"If I know Haley Gates," Dodie muttered, "he's probably face down in the hay in somebody's barn." Then she reached for the leather handle of a carpetbag. "I'm taking this back inside."

Emily jerked the bag away. "You'll do no such thing. I'm going, Dodie. And that's that."

"To Texas!" The young woman threw up her hands. "Texas! Where you'll be set upon by wild Indians. Maybe even scalped. Lord knows any savage would love to whack off those blond curls of yours."

"I'll be sure and keep my bonnet tied tight, then." Emily peered down the street in the opposite direction. "I'll scalp that Haley if he's not here in two more minutes."

Dodie sighed mightily, then sank into a high-backed wicker chair. "Elliot's going to be beside himself when he gets back from New Orleans to find you've taken off like some thief in the night. You know that, don't you? He'll be furious. He feels so responsible for you."

"It's ten o'clock in the morning, Dodie, and I'm not a thief. I'm not a prisoner, either. At least not anymore."

"A prisoner! What a spiteful thing to say, Emily, when all we've done is look out for your best interests since Mother and Father Russell passed away. Why, I'm sure those two must be fairly twirling in their graves right now, seeing what their foolish, dreamy daughter is up to."

Emily almost laughed at that image of her prim and

proper parents. But Dodie was probably right. If they knew what she was doing, her parents would most definitely spin in their shady little graves. As for being dreamy... Well, Dodie was probably right about that, too. But Emily wasn't foolish. Not now, at least.

Dodie sighed again, louder and longer. "Oh, how I wish that nice Mr. Gibbons hadn't gotten the croup and died. He was going to propose marriage, Emily. After all those years I simply knew he'd worked up the courage to pop the question. I could see it in his eyes."

"Perhaps," Emily said. And she would have married Alvin Gibbons, too, she thought. She would have had to marry him, and then they would have lived unhappily ever after. Only now her longtime, flesh-and-blood suitor was dead and Emily was on her way to Texas to find a man she didn't know in the flesh, but in letters. All those lovely letters.

"I'd like to scalp that no-good Price McDaniel for luring you away like this," Dodie moaned.

"He didn't lure me." Emily almost laughed at her sister-in-law's melodramatic despair. If anybody deserved to be melodramatic and despairing right now, it was Emily herself. "Price doesn't even know I'm coming."

"Well, that's just fine and dandy. You're traveling five thousand miles to see a man—a traitor, by the way—who may or may not even be there when you arrive."

"It's not five thousand miles. And Price is not a

traitor. He did what he had to do, Dodie, to get out of that horrible Yankee prison camp. You know that.''

''He should have come home.''

Emily gave an indignant snort. ''To what sort of welcome?''

They had had this argument before, a hundred times perhaps during Emily's six-year correspondence with the self-exiled Price McDaniel. But what her sister-in-law failed to recognize was that, during those six years, Emily had fallen in love with the man. She hadn't told a soul, though.

Well, that wasn't quite true. She had *confessed her love to* Price in a ten-page, heart-felt letter she had written on New Year's Eve, then sealed and mailed with such high hopes on the first day of 1872.

If you think me bold and brazen, dearest Price, then I am guilty as charged. Your Emmy loves you and would even be so bold as to propose a life together in the flesh rather just on paper. Send for me, Price. Oh, my dearest. Marry me.

His response had arrived, like clockwork, as all his previous letters had, and she had opened it with a brimming heart and trembling hands only to read his bitterly fond and conclusive farewell.

Someday I hope you can forgive me for misleading you. Dearest Emmy, I will not write again.

That evening she had wept on Alvin Gibbon's shoulder, and he—suddenly not so shy—had consoled her gently, if not a bit too thoroughly, just two weeks before he sickened and died.

"For God's sake," Dodie exclaimed now. "You barely knew Price when he was here and you haven't heard a word from him in months. How do you know he's still in Texas? How do you know he's still alive? Or that he even wants to see you?"

"I know," Emily lied, when what she knew was only that she had to leave. Today. Now. It wouldn't be long before everyone in Russell County knew that she—poor Emily, the dreamy spinster, the maiden lady whose shy suitor had passed away—was going to have a child.

Haley Gates had a tendency to spit when he talked, in part from his habit of dipping snuff and in part from the absence of front teeth, so while Emily sat beside him on the wagon seat, she was glad he kept his face forward and his eyes on the backsides of his mules. She was glad, too, that he had lapsed into silence after an hour-long discourse on who was up to what in Russell County. The man took extraordinary pleasure in pawing through almost everybody's dirty laundry. Almost everybody. Her own secret, she supposed, was still safe.

But if he said one more time just how brave she was for going out West alone, Emily couldn't decide whether she was going to hit him or to ask him to turn the wagon around and take her home. She didn't feel brave. She felt sick and scared to death.

Even so, there was no going back. Her decision wasn't based so much on the scandal her family would have to endure or her own sorry future as a fallen woman, but on the pitiful prospects for a child born out of wedlock in an unforgiving community.

She glanced at the unfortunate man beside her. Haley Gates was nearly forty years old, but tongues still wagged about his illegitimate origin, and more people than not referred to him as Sally Gates's bastard boy.

That wouldn't happen to her child, by God. He or she was going to have a chance in this unforgiving world. Emily meant to see to that, no matter how sick or scared she felt. No matter how ashamed she felt for closing her eyes that night and pretending Alvin Gibbons was the man she loved, that his hands were Price McDaniel's hands, that his kisses were the ones she craved, and that he loved her as desperately as she loved him.

"...friends or kinfolk?"

With a jolt, Emily realized that Haley had been speaking to her and she hadn't comprehended a single word he'd said. She apologized.

"Oh, that's all right, Miss Emily. A mind tends to wander on a pretty day like this." He spat, this time intentionally, over the side of the wagon. "I was just asking who you planned on visiting in Texas. I didn't know any Russells had ever left the county.''

"Only my uncle Randolph," she said. "And he went east to Washington, D.C.''

"So you're visiting a friend, then?''

"Yes. A friend.''

What did it matter now, telling Haley the truth? she wondered. Knowing Dodie's proclivity for gossip, she was certain the entire Ladies' Aid Society already knew her destination. And if the venerable LAS knew, then everybody in seven counties was sure to know within a week.

"I've been corresponding with Price McDaniel," she said as matter-of-factly as she could. "He chose to stay out West after the war to raise cattle. And he's cordially invited me to visit his ranch.''

Haley took one hand from the reins in order to scratch his head. "McDaniel. McDaniel. That doesn't strike any particular bell.''

"Well, he's been gone for quite some time. He had no sisters or brothers, and his parents passed away several years ago. They lived in that big white house on Solomon Street.''

"Oh, those McDaniels." Haley slapped his knee. "I remember them, all right. Why, I even helped carry out all that furniture they shipped to Texas.''

"Yes. I remember, too.''

What Emily remembered was slipping an envelope into a drawer of an enormous walnut desk, and then a month later being surprised by a thoughtful reply, written in a bold and quite masculine hand. The tone of the letter had been serious and almost poetic, which surprised her even more, because her memory of Price had been of a laughing and rather cavalier young man, given more to pranks than poetry.

How the war had changed him, she had thought at the time, and then with each successive letter, she found herself increasingly glad that the callow youth she recalled had been forged into such a strong yet gentle man.

Then, month by month, letter by letter, Emily had fallen in love. It had been her distinct impression, even her devout belief, that Price's feelings for her were of an equal depth and weight. *Dear Miss Russell* had long ago been replaced by *Dear,* then *Dearest Emily.* The second to the last letter—the one to which she had responded with such candor and passion— had begun *My Dearest Emmy.*

That one—the last one with half its inked words dripping down the pages from her happy tears—was now wrapped in a lace hanky and tucked deep inside the reticule on her lap. Price's other letters, tied with silk ribbons, a different color for every year, were secure in her leather valise. And although she had packed most of her clothes and other belongings for the trip to Texas, nothing really mattered but the letters, which had come to be her most valuable possessions, indeed her only priceless worldly goods.

"All that furniture," Haley murmured, shaking his head. "I sure do remember that now that you mention it, Miss Emily. Wonder if all them dressers and desks and what-nots made it to Texas all right. Did you ever hear?''

Emily smiled wistfully. ''The desk arrived, Haley. That's all I know for sure.''

The levee in Vicksburg was crowded when they arrived later that afternoon. Haley's mule-drawn wagon wasn't the worst-looking vehicle at the steamboat landing, but it didn't rank far above most of the produce wagons parked there. For one bleak moment, Emily felt that she had come down a peg or two in the world—until she reminded herself of her fallen status. She decided she was lucky indeed to even be able to afford a wagon ride, not to mention the passage she had booked on the *Memphis Zephyr,* whose smokestacks were already billowing with steam.

''I must hurry, Haley,'' she said, clambering down from the wagon seat before he could come to her aid, then reaching for the valise that held her precious letters. ''If you'll carry my other bags to the gangplank, I'd be most appreciative.''

Emily hurried across the cobblestones to show her ticket to the captain.

He squinted at her from beneath the polished brim of his cap. ''You traveling alone, Miss Russell?''

After she nodded, the man handed her ticket back, then lightly touched her arm. ''I'll keep a special eye out for you. Fine family, those people of yours. I've met your uncle, the legislator, on one or two occasions.''

"How nice," she replied while thinking that her Uncle Randolph would likely be the first to disown her in light of her condition.

"You give him my regards when next you see him, will you?''

"Indeed I will, Captain.''

"Is that your man with your luggage?'' he asked, angling his head toward Haley, who was just then waging a losing battle with a small steamer trunk, a suitcase and two carpetbags.

The Captain gestured to one of his crewmen, a muscular man. "See that Miss Russell's luggage makes it to her stateroom, will you?''

Then, after the Captain turned to greet other passengers, Emily walked back to bid farewell to Haley. He stood, gazing forlornly at the ground, the worn toe of one boot lodged between two cobblestones.

"Well, I guess it's time for you to get on board,'' he said. Then he looked up and gave her a wide but toothless grin. "I kinda wish I was going with you, Miss Emily. Out West, you know. Where things is all brand-new.''

"Brand-new,'' she echoed despite the lump in her throat, suddenly feeling far sorrier for Haley than she did for herself. "Well, come along then,'' she said, surprising herself by how much she meant it. "Come West with me where things are indeed all brand-new.''

Haley toed the cobblestones again. "It's tempting, Miss Emily. But there's my ma back in Russell County, you know. She's doing poorly, and I think she'd just plain up and die if I left her."

Emily was so touched by the man's loyalty to his mother that her eyes brimmed with tears. *You're a lucky woman, Sally Gates,* she thought, *and your bastard boy turned out to be your blessing, didn't he? I hope I'm just as fortunate.*

"Haley, I know I was only supposed to pay you six bits for the ride." Emily dug in her reticule as she spoke. "But, here. I want you to take this." She pressed a five dollar gold piece in his hand.

"Aw, Miss Emily. That's too much."

The *Memphis Zephyr*'s steam whistle gave three long, shrieking blasts, nearly deafening Emily.

"I said that's way too much," Haley shouted.

"I must run or I'll miss my boat." She bunched up her skirts and began to hasten toward the gangplank, then called back over her shoulder. "You keep that, Haley. Buy something nice for your mama."

"That's awful nice of you, Miss Emily. You have a safe trip now and you enjoy all them brand-new things out West, you hear? When you come home, I hope you'll tell me all about 'em."

"I'll do that, Haley," she lied, trying to smile through the tears and waving from the deck while the steamboat's gangplank rose as if it, too, were waving a long and last goodbye to Mississippi and everyone in it.

Harlequin is proud to introduce:

HEART OF THE WEST

...Where Every Man Has His Price!

Lost Springs Ranch was famous for turning young mavericks into good men. Word that the ranch was in financial trouble sent a herd of loyal bachelors stampeding back to Wyoming to put themselves on the auction block.

This is a brand-new 12-book continuity, which includes some of Harlequin's most talented authors.

Don't miss the first book,
Husband for Hire by **Susan Wiggs.**
It will be at your favorite retail outlet in July 1999.

HARLEQUIN®
Makes any time special ™

Look us up on-line at: http://www.romance.net   PHHOW

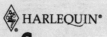

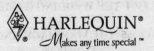

COMING NEXT MONTH FROM

HARLEQUIN HISTORICALS